I0650396

William Knighton

Elihu Jan's Story

Or, the private life of an eastern queen

William Knighton

Elihu Jan's Story
Or, the private life of an eastern queen

ISBN/EAN: 9783337323158

Printed in Europe, USA, Canada, Australia, Japan

Cover: Foto ©Andreas Hilbeck / pixelio.de

More available books at **www.hansebooks.com**

ELIHU JAN'S STORY

OR

THE PRIVATE LIFE OF AN EASTERN QUEEN

BY

WILLIAM KNIGHTON, LL.D.

ASSISTANT COMMISSIONER IN OUDH:

AUTHOR OF 'PRIVATE LIFE OF AN EASTERN KING,' 'VILLAGE LIFE IN OUDH,'

ETC.

LONDON:

LONGMAN, GREEN, LONGMAN, ROBERTS, & GREEN.

1865.

The right of translation is reserved.

PREFACE.

Eliⅈu Jan is not a fictitious character. She was brought up in the Court of Lucknow from her seventh year, as related in the first chapter of the following work. She was for many years hookah attendant to the queen of Oudh, and of course thus became acquainted with much that happened in the palace. After the mutiny, she was first an ayah in the household of Mr. Johannes, the wealthy merchant of Lucknow, and subsequently entered my wife's service in the same capacity. She has been with us now nearly three years, is still in our service, and, so far as I have been able to verify her accounts of the queen's private life, I have found them to be true. I therefore believe the truth of the whole, and I have narrated it as much as possible in her own words, and with her own reflections—allowances being made for the translation from Urdu into English.

HIMALAYA CLUB, MUSSOORIE:
June 1864.

CONTENTS.

ELIHU JAN'S STORY.

CHAPTER I.

PERSONAL REMINISCENCES.

THE earliest thing I can remember is that
my father, Ashabad Khan, lived with his
two brothers in our village, long, long ago,
some fifteen or sixteen miles from Lucknow.
The cottage was divided into three tenements,
each of which had its separate door, and was
shut off from the rest by its own partition
wall. The lands the three brothers cultivated
were crown lands, belonging to the king at
Lucknow, and it was not without difficulty
that the rent was paid. It was not the rent
alone that made the difficulty, but the
exactions of the various king's servants,
who claimed sums as their rights over and

B

4)

above the rent, which my father and uncles were afraid to refuse them. My mother had died at my birth, and my only female companion was a cousin, the daughter of a younger brother of my father, who was five or six years older than I, and who took care of me.

At length, what with exactions, and what with bad crops, things went from bad to worse, and one year the Sepoys came down upon us to force my father and uncles to pay the rents due, for they were much in arrears. My father and uncles ran away, and I and my cousin were taken off as slaves to the palace in Lucknow. I was about seven years of age, and I am an old woman now of near thirty, but I cannot tell exactly how old I am, or how old I was. This I know, that my father was a good Soonny * Mussulman, and that at the court they brought me up as a Sheeah ; but I have always been an unhappy creature—unhappy and miserable— since the time when I killed my mother at

* The Soonnies are the Protestants ; the Sheeahs, the Roman Catholics of Moslemism.

my birth. What luck or good fortune can the child expect that kills its mother?

Arrived at the palace, we were washed and dressed, and taken into the queen's apartments. I was speechless with astonishment at the grandeur of the rooms. The ceiling was beautifully painted, the walls were richly ornamented with large mirrors and gilt edgings. Chandeliers hung from the roof, and the floor was covered with a large carpet, and in the centre of the carpet was a white cloth. Upon the upper end of this white cloth was a smaller and richer carpet, with cushions, and a large pillow for the back gorgeously trimmed with thick gold fringe. The cushions were covered with crimson velvet, with flowers of gold thread worked on them. With her back leaning against the large round pillow sat the queen smoking her hookah. She was dressed in light-coloured clothes, all of one colour. She preferred light blue, lavender, or straw-coloured garments, with rich embroidery, and she wore much jewellery, nose-rings, ear-rings, bracelets, anklets, and such-like, all adorned profusely with precious stones. The queen was considered by us natives as very handsome; whether Europeans would think so or not, I do not know, for your ways and thoughts are not as ours. She was of the middle height, and at that time light and cheerful; not gloomy and sorrowful, as she was afterwards, when the kingdom was taken away from her son, and when she went to London to see the English queen, and ask for her son's kingdom back again. She had many sorrows after that time. I speak of the time when her husband was alive and on the throne, and when she was young and happy. Her complexion, when I first saw her, was a clear yellow. She was thin and finely formed; her eyes large, black, and lustrous; her hair of a dark-brown, not black; her features prominent; and her hands and feet small and delicate. She grew fat, and lost her delicate fragile beauty long before she went to England. But I am speaking of long, long ago.

When we were first brought into the

queen's presence, my cousin and I, the queen
spoke kindly to us, and sent for sweetmeats.
But I could not eat, I was too busy gazing
around; all was new and beautiful to me; I
thought, surely this is Peristan (the country
of the Peris), and these are surely Peris, not
mortals. But I was told to eat, and I did
so, and found the sweetmeats so delicious,
that I soon forgot everything else. We were
asked whether we were Sheeahs or Soonnies,
and the queen was sorry to hear that we
were Soonnies. To me, ignorant as I was,
the difference was a small matter; but my
cousin was better instructed, and told me
afterwards I must always continue to be a
Soonny in heart, whatever they taught me.
I was well fed, and my duties were light, so
that I did not dislike living in the palace;
but it was not so with my cousin—she was
refractory, and was often punished.

A year passed away. I cannot remember
much of that far-off time. Good living and
light work made me fat and well-looking.
My father and his brothers had got money
enough to pay their debts, and came to

Lucknow to pay the money, and to reclaim my cousin and myself. My cousin was quite willing to go, but I was not so willing. When I was taken to see my father, who was waiting at the palace, I told him I did not want to go home. He was sorrowful, and lamented. I could not bear to see him so sad, and I said, Well, if I go home you must give me khoormas, pillaus, and curries, such as I get here to eat; not khodo, and dhall, as I got at home before. When the queen heard that I was not willing to go home she sent for me again and spoke kindly to me : her heart was good. She sent word to my father that I should be brought up at the palace and taught to prepare her hookah, and that he might come occasionally to see me. But my father was not content, and one day when the king, Umjid Aly Shah, was going through the streets of Lucknow in his janpan or chair, my father threw himself on the ground before him, and begged for justice and mercy. The king asked what was the matter, and my father said he would die if his daughter were not restored to him, for she was his only child. The king promised to exert himself in the matter, and spoke to the queen. At first the queen refused, but afterwards consented, on condition that if, after some time, I still wished to return, I was to be allowed to do so. So I was taken home by my father and lived at home for several months—I cannot tell exactly how many months—but it was less than a year; some six or eight months perhaps.

I was not so happy at home as I had been in the palace. My father was seldom with me, and my cousin was not kind, and the neighbours knew that I had killed my mother at my birth, miserable that I am, and so I longed to return. At length one day two Chuprassies came from Lucknow, and said the queen wanted to see me, and I was brought back to the court. She asked me if I wished to remain at home, or would prefer being her slave. I spoke as a child; I preferred the palace to our poor cottage, and I was not allowed to return to my father; nor did he come to reclaim me, wretched that I am: he loved me no longer.

Another year passed away, and the queen was kind, and a Moollah was appointed to teach us the Koran. We learned something of it, but we often bribed the Moollah to let us play in the courtyard where the fountains were, instead of being taught. There were six or eight of us, all about the same age— nine or ten years of age—some good some bad, some pretty some ugly, as the way of the world and of mankind is. We bribed the Moollah with money, or ornaments, or sweetmeats, or whatever we had. He was an old white-bearded man, we were slaves; what did he care whether we learned or not? But all we learned was Sheeah doctrine and Sheeah customs, and to this day I know no other. I was always a castaway. At length it was told the queen that we were not learning but playing, and she sent for us one day to hear what we could read and repeat, and we knew little or nothing. So the queen was angry, and sent to the Moollah to say her slaves were not learning, and next day the Moollah beat us all with a cane, and in the evening we went to the

queen and begged mercy and justice, and
showed her the marks of the cane, and she
said, ' Wah! wah! what trouble it is—it is
not their fate to learn—let the Moollah be
dismissed.' She was a kind queen and a
good always.

It was shortly after the dismissal of the
Moollah that news was brought of my father
being on his death-bed, and the queen
ordered me to be taken to see him. I suppose I was about ten years of age, but how
can I tell exactly? Is it that all my life is
written down in a book, that I should be
able to tell exactly how old I was when
each thing happened?

I found my father lying on his bed with
closed eyes. I thought he was dead at first.
But after a little, he opened his eyes and
saw me and knew me. Many were there;
my cousin and others attending on him. He
feebly lifted his arms to embrace me. I laid
my head beside his head, and wept. Miserable that I was and am, I knew then that I
had no mother, and my father was going,
and I was to be a slave—an outcast from

my family and my religion—alone in the world, and unhappy always. But who shall avoid their fate? God gives to one happiness and to another misery, and who shall question it? I thought my father was trying to speak to me: perhaps he was, but he was weak, and his head turned from mine on the pillow, and they said ' He will sleep;' so I arose, and took off my muslin head-dress, and covered his face with it, and sat near the door watching. Three or four hours passed away. My cousin and the others had gone; I was alone with my sleeping father, and I was very wretched, but my heart was too full for tears'; I could not cry. I was afraid and sad. At length they came enquiring one by one. I said ' He sleeps,' but they lifted the covering from his face, and said ' He is dead.'

I now knew what it was to be alone indeed. Born wretched, I have lived wretched. Such has been my fate. I was too stupefied for tears, and my former companions and playmates crowded round me, and watched me, and said, ' She does not cry;

do not the Sheeahs weep for dead fathers?'
I was treated as an outcast; I deserved to
be so treated. I was not fit to eat with my
relatives, all good Soonnies; I was not allowed to sit on the same mat with them. I
could not use the same vessels for cooking.
I was a Sheeah, and I was glad to get back
again to court, where all were Sheeahs, and
where the queen was kind. I learned to
rub the queen's feet, and to prepare her
hookah, and I was as happy as so miserable
and forlorn a creature as I can ever expect
to be.

But I was married? yes, of course I was
married. But God denied me children.
What right had I to expect children, who
had killed my mother at my birth? My
marriage was thus. When I was fit to be
married, the queen told me it was time, and
I was nothing loath. The news was told
that one of the queen's slave-girls was to be
married, and many men came forward to
offer. But the queen would have no Soonnies. At length a Sheeah, the son of a
Sheeah, offered—Gholam Hussain by name.

He was told to come into the courtyard one day at noon, and I saw him there. He did not see me. I was with other girls, and one of them, whom I had offended a few days before, caught hold of my arm, and said to another girl, 'That is to be Elihu Jan's husband. Behold, she carries her head high and is proud, and God has sent her a husband as black as an Abyssinian.' I had no choice in the matter; all was arranged for me. Gholam Hussain got a shop for selling tobacco and such-like, near the palace gates, and I was married to him. I did not like him at first, and spent as much time as I could away from him, in attendance on the queen. But he was kind to me, and I liked him better at last; and although he is black, he is not a bad man. But I was fated to misery.

After the queen's husband, Umjid Aly Shah, had died, and his son Wajid Aly Shah had reigned many years, then the English came and took the kingdom, and the queen, my mistress, mother of the king, said, 'I will go to England. The Queen of England is also

a mother. I will ask her to give me back
my kingdom.' Alas! what wailing, what
sorrow, what beating of breasts, then took
place amongst us! 'How shall you cross
the great black seas?' said we, 'you, who
fear even the river?' But it was fate, and
she said she would go, and she went. I
went with her to Calcutta, and my husband
was with us. The king offered to support
us in Calcutta, for the queen, his mother,
charged him to be kind to all her attendants.
But I would not live in *his* palace; I would
prefer begging my bread abroad in the
world. I returned to Lucknow with my
husband. We lived on my jewels and ornaments for some time. My husband's shop
was cleared away. All the bazaar was
cleared away. The English like grass better
than bazaars. God has given them the kingdom. God's will be done. But when the
gold and silver ornaments, and my few
jewels, were all eaten up, then I became a
servant. The English ladies are kind and
good, and they believe in God, and I love
my mistress, that is, ever since the queen

died in Europe.   And my husband? oh! he is as black as ever, a good kind man, and he sits at home and eats opium, and smokes the hookah.   My wages are enough for both of us.

CHAPTER II.

THE QUEEN'S DAILY LIFE.

DURING the life of her husband, Umjid Aly
Shah, the queen was very happy. She had
been his only wife for many years, and the
first serious quarrel between them was when
he took a second wife. At first the queen
knew nothing of it, but, when she came to
hear of it, she refused to see the king for
three days, and abstained from eating, and
was silent, until the vizier and officers of
state represented to her that serious injury
would result to the kingdom if she persevered
in so doing. Still, she was always the chief
queen. She was the mother of the heir-
apparent, the present ex-King of Oudh,
Wajid Aly Shah, and after Umjid Aly Shah's
death, the honours paid to her as queen-
dowager, and as mother of the king, were

similar to those she received during her husband's lifetime.

The queen and Umjid Aly Shah were fond of each other, and she led a virtuous, religious life always, whatever might be going on in the palace or city, or however her husband or son might act. But men are always great evil-doers, and when women have power, and are able to live as they choose, all is moral and regular. It is the power and influence of men that cause the evil. One wife, four wives, fifty wives will not suffice a king, whilst a queen is content with one husband, if he will but be faithful. But when was man ever faithful?

I was only a child when Umjid Aly Shah was king, and I did not see so much of the queen then, as I did afterwards during the reign of her son, Wajid Aly. Can I remember in those far-off days what she said or what she did? I was a child, and it is long long ago; but this I know, that she was always kind and good.

She was fond of the Chutter Munzil and the Chowlukhy Palaces in Lucknow, and of Dwarka Dhass' garden-house in the country.

These were her three favourite residences.
During the cold weather she usually resided
in the Chutter Munzil, and it was a common
thing for her to sit at one of the windows, looking out through the venetians at the river and
the road, watching whatever was passing there;
and often did she send for some poor crying
woman, and send her away with comfort in her
heart and money in her hand. The Chowlukhy
she preferred in the hot season, and the garden-
house in the rains. I remember once I was
waiting on her during the rains, when she
had come in for a few days to the Chutter
Munzil, and she was looking out on the
swollen river whilst I was attending to her
hookah. She called out to me, ' Elihu Jan,
there is an old woman being carried down
the river! Run, call the attendants — get
assistance—have her saved!' I ran and
called out for help. The poor old woman's
cottage had been swept away by the flood, and
she was holding on to part of the thatched roof
as it was being carried along. She was soon
released by the help of the attendants despatched for the purpose, and having been

dried and clothed, she was brought into the queen's apartment. After learning her his- tory, and that the poor old woman was alone in the world, all her relatives dead, none to help or comfort or support her, the queen settled a pension of three rupees a month on her. She used to go about Lucknow afterwards, always called the 'floating old woman' by the crowd, and I saw her so going about shortly before the English took the country. What became of her then, how can I tell? When the world was turned upside down, and kings and queens lost their thrones, what matter what became of one poor old woman?

To the garden-house there was a large garden attached, with high walls all round; and during the rainy season, when it was pleasantly cool between the showers, the queen, with her attendant women, a hundred of them, or two hundred of them, would roam round the walks, enjoying herself like a child. With a good heart and a propitious fate one may be very happy anywhere, but particularly in a garden, for the flowers and trees remind one of Paradise.

The queen was very religious. After rising about ten or eleven o'clock in the morning, she usually had her hands and face washed by her attendants, tasted a little unleavened cake with a preparation of milk, and then went to her dressing-room, where the Moollah always attended to read the Koran —the Moollah being separated from her by a screen. After her husband's death she used to read the Koran herself far into the night, for she was a great scholar, and her words were wise. A cooling drink was brought to her in hot weather before the mid-day meal, and this drink was of conserves and diluted pearls. All kings and queens, I have heard, drink diluted pearls, and it is said, moreover, that they are a very wholesome thing, and of great virtue; but of course none but kings and queens could afford to drink them. I had nothing to do with the queen's drinks or meats, only her hookah, and I rubbed her feet too; but I have no doubt she drank the pearls—everybody said she did.

After dressing and sitting in state, the midday meal or breakfast was introduced. The

queen's breakfast was cooked by women in
her own kitchens, the king's by men in other
kitchens. But often, with band playing, the
king came to eat with the queen, and his
breakfast was brought over on silver trays.
A cannon was fired at noon, and that was
the signal for breakfast. The second meal,
or dinner, was at or after sunset, and consisted of the same viands, pillaus of three
kinds, khoormas, kabobs, strong broths of
meat or sheep's head, with all kinds of
vegetables, and sweetmeats. Can I remember all she ate, when twenty to thirty
dishes were introduced at each meal? She
always ate with a spoon, not with her hands
as we do. The hookah was introduced after
each meal, and, if people came for an audience
after that, it was well for them if the king's
or the queen's hookah was properly prepared. The best of people are cross if their
food or their hookah is bad, but particularly
if the hookah is not properly prepared.

On retiring to rest the queen always had
a story-teller, to narrate something to her.
When the king was alive, the story-teller used
to sit behind a screen, not far from the bed,

but when she became a widow, the story-teller
sat at the bed's head, and varied her story
according to the queen's taste. If the object
was to induce sleep, a drowsy, monotonous,
rigmarole story, drawlingly told, soon pro-
duced the desired effect. If the object was to
amuse, to excite, to enliven, to soothe sorrow,
the story-teller varied her tale accordingly.
Far into the night the tale was told, and a
handsome present was the reward of a really
good story. There were four favourite story-
tellers. The attendants were changed as the
story-teller was introduced, and as she left
they were changed again. The queen was
fond of stories, and often told some to us, but
chiefly religious stories. The tales told by
the story-tellers were of all kinds: about
kings and queens, about love—about beggars
becoming princes, or princes beggars—about
the Peris and the Court of Indra. There are
plenty of story-tellers left in Lucknow, if you
want to know what kind of tales they told.

When the queen bathed, then was there
much preparation, and a long and tiresome
day's work for her servants. I was not one
of the bath attendants, but I know all about

it. Cisterns of cold water were filled in the humaum, and pipes of warm water, all were got ready betimes, and on the day for bathing both the queen and her attendants prepared for a hard day's work. Soap was not used in the queen's bath, but *basun* (ground pease) instead. Two or three of the oldest attendants, who had been with the queen from her maidenhood, attended, undressed, and bathed her. *Basun* was plentifully rubbed over each limb, and washed off with warm water, rubbed on and washed off, over and over again, perhaps twenty times—a tedious process. The queen and her attendants were all equally tired before the bath was over, and by that time the usual meal was ready. There were eunuchs, of course, in the palace—what palace is without them?—but the queen did not like them, and they only appeared on occasions of public ceremony, processions, and such-like. They had nothing to do with the bath. There were women-soldiers also, on guard in uniform and with musket, bayonet, &c., at the entrances of the female apartments of the palace, and in the corridors. The queen did not like them, and interfered little with them. The old customs were maintained, but with as little parade as possible. In fact, so averse was the queen to parade and fuss, that she seldom went abroad, except when it was absolutely necessary. The collection of elephants, camels, and horses, cavalry and foot-soldiers, silver-stick bearers, and guards of all kinds, was a bore to her. She liked elegant dresses and neat jewellery, but she was wearied with state apparel, and often, on returning from expeditions of ceremony, would throw herself down tired on the couch, exclaiming, 'Let them all go away: bismillah! but I am glad it is all over, it is very tiresome.' After her husband's death she never wore the nose-ring again, but retained all her other jewels and state apparel. A band preceded her, and guards and troops attended when she was queen-dowager, just as when she was queen-regnant; for was she not the king's mother?

For exercise and amusement the grounds, enclosed by high walls, near the palaces and at the country-seats of the king, were sufficient. There were artificial fountains, and sheets of water, and flowers and fruit-trees, and well-kept walks; ample space for walk-

ing or riding or driving, as the humour
might be. The queen did not ride on horse-
back ; modest women in our country never
do. The manners of Europeans are different ;
in all things God has made the two people
different. The queen made long journeys in
a silver howdah on an elephant, or in her
state palanquin, or tonjon, carried by slaves in
red liveries.

In the house a room was always set apart
for dining, and used for no other purpose.
There were no large tables, and high chairs
in it, as in the Sahibs' dining-rooms, but small
tables were brought in with the entertainment, on which the silver dishes were placed ;
and the queen sat on her usual cushions, with
a large richly-embroidered pillow at her
back, as at the durbar. Her arms and face
were washed after each meal, for she was
scrupulously clean. Even the small tables or
stools for the reception of the dishes were
often of pure silver, and the floor was covered with the richest carpets. Chandeliers
hung from the ceiling, and large mirrors with
gilt frames covered the walls. The royal
dustar khwan, or table cloth, was composed

of two large pieces of handsome broad cloth, designed in patterns of flowers, and ornamental devices, covering a piece of leather of equal size, sewn up all round. The tablecloth was spread in the centre of the apartment at dinner-time, and all the dinner apparatus was placed on it. Much ice was used, both for cooling sherbets, and the hookah-water. The queen drank no wine or strong drinks. As to the king, how can I tell what he drank in his own apartments? but when with the queen he drank nothing but sherbets, and such drinks as a Mussulman is allowed to drink.

There were several drawing-rooms in each palace. The centre was usually occupied by a round table, of rare woods, or marble, or crystal, or silver-gilt, and on this were placed ornaments of all kinds, china, gold, silver, lacquered ware, vases, and clocks. The ornaments came from China, from Delhi, and from Europe.* Couches, of the European fashion, covered with rich bright damask or silk, were also to be found in the drawing-rooms ; and,

---

* Many of them from Birmingham.

in each such room, one bed was always ready-made for reclining upon in the day-time, covered with some rich counterpane.

The dressing-rooms had the usual mirrors and chandeliers, with boxes all round the room for clothes and jewellery—not presses, or almirahs, or chests of drawers, as European ladies have. The furniture of the bed and bath-room was all of pure silver. There were also two golden bedsteads in the palace, which the ex-king took with him to Calcutta.*

The queen's treasury was guarded by soldiers, and there was an apartment adjoining it, called the *tykhanah*, not an underground apartment, for retiring to in very warm weather, as the word usually means, but a storehouse for spare clothes, jewels, and such-like. In this *tykhanah* there was one large box full of a mixture of rupees and gold mohurs, called *khichry*, from the dish of that name. It had been filled and placed there by Umjid

---

* These golden bedsteads were made in the time of Saadut Aly Khan, and it is said that one of them has been melted down recently in Calcutta, by order of the ex-king.

Aly's father, and was only to be used in time of extraordinary need. All this was spent in the reign of her son, the ex-king, Wajid Aly Shah. Once when the queen was away at the garden-house, for a fortnight or so, some of the female slaves left behind broke into this room, and succeeded in opening one of the boxes of jewels. A girl of about sixteen years of age, whom the queen had promised in marriage to an attendant of the king, was the ringleader in this theft. The queen had been very kind to her, and it was a case of signal ingratitude. Only one box had been opened, and that so unskilfully, that great injury had been done to the jewels within. The property had been taken from it during the night, and next morning traces of the burglary and of the theft were apparent. The queen was informed of it, and returned to Lucknow. Suspicion fell upon the slave-girl in question, and she was scourged with canes upon the back, until she confessed. She pointed out in what places in Lucknow the property would be found, and a good deal of it was recovered, but much injured in value.

The queen usually gave audience between the morning and evening meals. Distressed women from the country of all classes would come to her, with petitions, with complaints, with presents. She was ready to hear them all, to do the best she could for all. It was a source of great gain to us her servants, for none got an audience without paying handsomely for it. Whoever came was kept waiting, and put off from day to day, with various excuses, until we thought we could get nothing more out of them, and then, and not till then, were they admitted—just as the native clerks and others do in the Sahibs' Kucherry, where the Sahibs administer justice. Would the poor people not complain? you ask. Of course not. Do they complain at Kucherry? Is it not the custom? Will the word of one stranger be believed before that of twenty servants? Well, perhaps it was wrong. But it is the custom of this country. God has made Europeans different. You cannot change the nature of man.

CHAPTER III.

THE SKELETON IN THE CLOSET.

EVERYBODY has some enemies, and, good and religious as our queen was, she too had her enemies. These were chiefly the low-born women whom her son married when he became king. It was customary, when the son wished to contract a new marriage, to send the bride to the queen-mother for her approval first. My mistress objected to some, but he took them into his harem all the same ; and when she found her remonstrances and her opposition useless, she ceased to object to any of them, approving of all he sent. He had all kinds of wives. Some of them princesses to whom he had been married in his father's lifetime, but when he became king he had black women, Abyssinians, high caste and low, young and old,

Mussulman and Hindu, all kinds of women for wives; and my mistress never recognised and never acknowledged any of them as queens, except the high-born princesses to whom he had been first married.

The chief wife of Wajid Aly, and the mother of the heir-apparent, had not ceremonial honours, and was not attended by a state equal to that of my mistress, and this was the cause of much ill-feeling. Several attempts were made on my mistress's life, and they were all traced to the harem of the king, her son.

Umjid Aly Shah had died of an ulcer, or some such sore on his shoulder, and I have heard the queen, my mistress, say that the sore must have been poisoned by some one, most probably by one of the physicians, bribed by some one who benefited most by his death. Had Umjid Aly Shah lived, I have no doubt the crime would have been found out, and the criminal discovered; but when he died, who was going to tell? who would protect the physician who asserted poison had been used? what witnesses would

come forward against the instigator of the
crime, when that man the instigator was
all-powerful? Umjid Aly Shah had warned
the queen not to allow Wajid Aly to ascend
the throne in case he, Umjid Aly, died; but
what could she do? She was but a woman.
Wajid Aly was the eldest son, and the English Resident, who knew nothing of palace
wives perhaps, declared that the eldest son
must succeed. And so Wajid Aly became
king, and the fate of Oudh was bad, for the
wickedness of Lucknow was great. How
do I know that? Does not every one know
that Lucknow was as the cities that God
burnt up once for wickedness? Is it not
written in the Koran?

I do not say that Wajid Aly poisoned his
father, or that Khash Mehal, his chief wife,
tried to murder the queen, my mistress;
but I do say that, in the palace, such things
were spoken of, and many of the slaves
believed such stories to be truths. 'Would
a son murder his father? would a daughter-
in-law attempt the life of her mother-in-law?'
These were the questions I would ask, and

they would reply, ' A kingdom is at stake—
the prize is great—God is good, but Lucknow is very wicked.'

I know that, if she could, my mistress
would have placed her second son, whom
we called the General Sahib, because he was
commander-in-chief, on the throne.   But
the English would have the eldest son, Wajid
Aly ; and so Wajid Aly was crowned, and
now Oudh is no longer a kingdom.   But
what have I to do with making of kings and
queens, and raising and upsetting kingdoms ?
I am but a slave, or rather I was but a slave,
and I can only tell what I saw and heard.

During the Mohurrim all the chief servants got mingled together in the ceremonial
visits of the king's family.   Khash Mehal's
servants, and Wajid Aly's, and we, all met
in the various palaces often, during the Mohurrim, for ceremonial visits were then frequent and usual.   It was, then, during the
Mohurrim that I was one day preparing the
queen's hookah, as usual, in the Chutter
Munzil Palace.   I cannot tell what year it
was ; what had I to do with years and dates ?

but it was five or six years before the English took the kingdom. It was my custom
before putting on the mouthpiece, and taking
the hookah to the queen, to put my own mouth
to the end of the snake,* and draw it for
a few minutes, so as to ignite the tobacco
thoroughly. I was doing so on this occasion,
when I felt some fine tasteless powder drawn
up into my mouth, for which I could not
account. I had cleaned the snake thoroughly in the morning, and at first I
thought ashes from the chillum, or bowl,
had got through ; but that was impossible, as
the smoke was drawn through the water. I
fortunately did not swallow the powder, but
spat it out. I suspected poison at once, and
went to the queen to tell her so. She only
laughed at me, and said to her attendant,
'Go, and see what strange mare's nest the
unfledged wit of Elihu Jan has discovered.'
I showed the attendant some of the white
impalpable dust, and she had the hookah
snake carefully cut open. The white powder

* The long elastic tube of the hookah is called the
'snake.'

D

was discovered scattered over the tube inside. How do I know how they got it there? Those who do the devil's work will get assistance from the devil, I suppose. But there it was, plain and unmistakable. Very fine, and very thinly scattered; all that was loose I had drawn up. A hakeem, or physician, was called by the queen to examine the powder, and he said it was poison, and advised that I should be punished—may evil light on the grey beard of him!—but the queen was good and just, and said, 'No, no! this is not Elihu Jan's doing; my enemy hath done this.' Can I tell who she meant was her enemy? Yes, I could guess. That enemy is still alive in Calcutta—the chief wife of the ex-king—Khash Mehal. But the queen may have been mistaken, of course. There was no proof. The English want proofs of everything, as if people called witnesses to watch them attempt to poison a queen. Mashallah! but the ways of the English are wonderful, and past all finding out.

Nor was that the only attempt of the

enemy. The bed, as I already mentioned, was always covered with a rich counterpane, and, when prepared for the night, was not turned down from the pillow, as we prepare the beds for the Sahibs. Often, particularly during the hot weather, the queen lay down *on* the counterpane, not *under* it, the attendants fanning her and brushing away the flies. It was again during the Mohurrim. The queen, wearied with the prayers and ceremonies of the morning, and with her rigid fast, came into her bedroom to lie down. She had a high pillow, so as to use the hookah without inconvenience, as she reclined. I was preparing the hookah, and was just in the act of carrying it into the room, when a great commotion arose in the bedroom. A snake, in a charmed or comatose state, was found coiled up under the counterpane, near the foot of the bed. A search was made, and outside was found the earthen jar in which the snake had been brought. The queen had the snake restored to the earthen jar, and then held a consultation as to what was best to be done. It could not have come there by accident. That was quite out of the question. The snake was a deadly cobra-di-capello, about three feet long.

Early next morning, by beat of drum, all the snake-charmers of Lucknow were ordered to attend at the queen's palace, and guards were sent round to collect them. As the snake that had been found in the queen's bed was in a charmed state, it was evident some of these men had been employed to charm it, and could give evidence on the subject. It was explained to them that no harm would happen from confession, as whoever was employed was doubtless kept in ignorance of the cause. But they all denied—liars they are and were. Those that discover crime and hidden things by ordeals and otherwise, were then called in, and they pointed out one of the snake-charmers, who looked frightened and confused, as the party who had charmed the snake. He still denied. But the queen was determined to make him confess. His back was bared. Ice was first rubbed over it, and then the rattan was applied. He got about twenty lashes, when

he offered to confess everything. The queen
was merciful, and his hands were removed
from the split bamboo in which they had been
placed, according to custom, when whipping
was administered. He was released, and confessed that he had charmed the snake. The
evening before, he said, the head darogah or
gate-keeper of one of the king's wives had
come to him, asking him to charm this snake,
so that it would lie perfectly still, wherever it
was placed, for eighteen or twenty hours, and
he had done so, and given the darogah back
the snake, and knew nothing more of the
matter. The darogah was called, and of
course denied it all—what else could be expected? But on collecting the servants who
had had access to the bedroom that morning,
the finders-out of crime by ordeal were again
called, and pointed out the maidservant who
had been bribed by the darogah to put the
snake into the queen's bed. She too denied.
Will the father of lies let his children speak
the truth? They were both flogged severely
—the darogah and the maidservant — and
thrown separately into prison, into under-

ground dungeons of one of the old palaces. The queen was merciful, and would not have them put to death, although the king, her son, advised her to have them both impaled. The snake-charmer was allowed to go free, but of course he will carry the marks of the scourging on his back all his life. The cane was not laid on lightly in the palace, you may be sure.

I have no doubt of the guilt of the darogah and the maidservant—none whatever. When the ordeal is used to discover crime, it is God who decides, not man. The girl was a slave like myself, but unmarried—not a bad-looking girl, very merry and lively, but too fond of ornaments. She sold herself for them, I dare say. What if the diviners of crime had pointed me out? you ask. If they had, I should have been scourged and imprisoned in the underground dungeon, full of rats and vermin. Yes, of course I should; but I tell you it was impossible. God is good. You want witnesses and proofs again. Wah! wah! witnesses and proofs may do for England, but we trust

in God. You could get fifty witnesses in
Lucknow at two annas (threepence) a day
to swear anything, in any way.* But why
should Khash Mehal wish for the queen-
mother's death? you ask. Why do people
like to be great and powerful? guards, attendants, a band, silver-sticks in waiting,
priority in all processions?—these were the
right of my mistress; and, if she was removed, Khash Mehal would have been the
first woman in Oudh. I know of no other
reason why she should wish the queen-mother
dead.

Even from her own daughter the queen
got but little sympathy. Her son, the
general, who accompanied her to England,
was her greatest friend, and him she could
trust in all things. The general had no easy
part to play in Lucknow. He had a very

---

* It is quite evident that there is nothing in either
of the above instances of attempted murder, if indeed
they were such, to prove the complicity of any of the
king's household, even as Elihu Jan relates the story.
Her strong impressions on the subject were doubtless
those of the household to which she was attached.

handsome wife, and he was afraid if his
brother the king saw her, he would take her
to himself. The king wanted to see her, but
the general never allowed her to come to
court, and changed her residence frequently,
and his mother, my mistress, helped him.
She loved the general much better than she
loved Wajid Aly, and the general was a
good man and just to woman.

The marriage of the queen's daughter with
Nawab Sath Chood Dowlah had not been a
happy one; and the queen sympathised with
her, and often remonstrated with the nawab.
Yet when the queen called on her daughter,
at the time of the Mohurrim, and told her of
this attempt on her life, the answer she got
was: 'Your life will do you little good at
your age. Are you not old? are not your
teeth gone? can you live long?' Perhaps
it was in the bitterness of her own heart
that the shahzadee (princess) so spoke, but
she was wrong so to speak. The queen was
angry, and ordered her chair forthwith,
without giving any reply, and went away,
and several months passed before there was

any reconciliation between them. She too, the shahzadee, would have taken a higher position if the queen, my mistress, died. From all I could find out, after living more than twenty years in a palace, there is less natural affection there than in the mud cabin where all are poor. But it is not right for a slave to judge the king or the royal family—the queen taught us that out of the Koran; and the hearts of princes are past finding out. Are we not all in hands of God?

CHAPTER IV.

MINOR TROUBLES.

THE real sorrows of the queen began with the death of her husband, Umjid Aly Shah, but she had apparent sorrows enough even when he was alive. He had been a long time heir apparent, and did not come to the throne till he was advanced in middle life, and only reigned five years. It was very shortly after his reign began that I was brought to the palace, and, child though I was, I remember everyone used to say he was a model of a husband, because he had never taken any other wife. The queen's children, three boys and one girl, were all born before her husband came to the throne.

The only apparently cruel thing I can remember the queen having ever done, was the result of jealousy. When Umjid Aly had been nearly a year or so on the throne, he began to distinguish one of the queen's attendant girls by presents, and by sending to her kind messages. As this girl was the servant usually in charge of the youngest prince, then an infant, the king had many opportunities of speaking to her, and the queen thought the presents he gave her were prompted by his affection for the child. The household, however, knew better, and began to treat her with more respect, and to call her by higher titles, when they saw that the king was really attached to her. Whether the king went through any ceremony of marriage with her, or not, I do not know. Certain it is, however, that the queen came to hear of the affection he displayed, and of the consequent assumption by her servant of titles of honour and a proud carriage, when not actually in the queen's presence.

Now the queen was known to all to be a resolute determined woman. She was learned, could read and write Persian and Arabic, was a princess of Delhi by birth and a queen by marriage—was such a woman to allow a base-born slave to step between her and her lord, she being the mother of the king's children? When she once expressed a desire for anything, she always got it, no matter who opposed. If it was not granted at once, she neither eat nor drank till either the request was granted, or at least a solemn promise was made to grant it. But she was wise too, and never injured the kingdom by her demands. Sole lord of the king's heart, mother of his children, was she to allow a rival to carry off his affections from her? Certainly not.

The attendant in question, I forget her name, was one afternoon sleeping soundly, fatigued by exercise, and overcome by the sultriness of the day. The apartment in which she slept was at the end of a gallery leading from the queen's private rooms to those of public reception. The queen accidentally passed by, and saw her there asleep. The attendant was a handsome girl, full grown, with a fine figure, and through some accident had never been married. It was whispered in the palace that she would one day be mother of a royal child, whether truly or falsely I do not know.

The queen passed on and said nothing till she came to her own apartment. She then called to her one of her most trusted servants—an old woman who had been with her from her maidenhood, who had come with her from Delhi. How the thing was managed afterwards I do not know, but soon all the palace was in an uproar, roused by the screams of the attendant who had been sleeping a few minutes before so soundly, dreaming perhaps of the affection of a king. She had been sleeping, I heard, with face and neck uncovered, the usual muslin veil having been thrown aside in consequence of the heat; and some description of firework, or explosive substance, had been let off so close to her as to burn her severely on the face and neck. The queen was very sorry for the pain she suffered, and was doing all she could to alleviate it, when the king came in. A dark scowl was on his face. The girl was removed by his orders, in order that proper medical aid might be obtained. She was long ill. Her beauty was clean gone for ever, and she was soon forgotten. I do not know what became of her afterwards.

I was only a child when all this happened, but I remember the screams and the bustle, and the queen's sorrow. She cried over the poor girl, her heart was good. It was never proved, of course, that she had anything to do with it, but I believe she had, all the same. There was an investigation, of course, and it was all set down as the result of accident; but they say that the king was for a long time terribly angry. His anger, however, was little matter, for the queen ruled him still. There was but one will between the two, and that will was hers.

But was not all this very cruel on the queen's part? No, not cruel, but in reality very merciful. Any other queen would have had the slave put to death, and her body thrown into the river. If I were a queen— well it's no use saying what I should do if I were a queen, but no slave should come between me and my husband. Of that you may be sure. Cruel? No, my mistress the queen was never cruel. She was pious and devout and charitable, and read the Koran daily. Had her husband and her son been as good as she was, God would never have taken the kingdom from the family. Was not all the fault in this case her husband's?

Yes, the king had his revenge nevertheless. He took a flower-girl of Lucknow, and married her by *muta* (an inferior or left-handed marriage peculiar to the Sheeahs). She had a palace given to her, and was made great and wealthy, but the queen knew nothing of it, as I heard, until cannon announced the birth of a son. When she subsequently reproached the king on the subject, his answer was, that in the Koran many more wives were allowed than he had ever taken or intended to take. Before all the servants she spoke loudly and bitterly in reply, saying, ' True, it is allowed, and you have waited till the best years of your life are gone, and now, in your old age, you take a flower-girl to wife—a flower-girl fresh from the bazaar. Your servants, who have bought flowers from her, are daily in your court, and say in their hearts, as they look on you, " Behold the husband of the flower-girl, from whom we bought flowers in the bazaar on such a day!"' The king rose and went away in a rage ; and the queen's attendants said to her, ' He will not come again.' 'He *shall* not come,' was her answer, but it was only in bravado she said it, for when she was in her own room she cried bitterly.

The young wife, the flower-girl, was called *mulika*, or princess, after the birth of her son, but never in the queen's presence, nor was that son ever spoken of before her as *sahib-alum*, or *sháhzadha*, or prince. Her servants and attendants well knew she would not allow it.

But, as I have said, Umjid Aly Shah only reigned a few years, and when he first fell ill he showed his affection for the queen my mistress throughout, till his death. I do not know what his sickness was. I only know he was sick, and that the immediate cause of death was an ulcer or sore on his shoulder, which gave him great pain, and which the

queen afterwards believed had been poisoned
by one of his physicians, bribed so to do, as I
have said before.

A few days before his death the mulika,
daughter of the fruiterer, sent her son, in
order that he might get his father's blessing.
She did not venture to come herself, for the
queen would never have given her permission
to enter her apartments, but she hoped there
would be mercy for her infant son, and she
was right. She knew the queen had a good
heart.

When the sahibalum came we knew not
how to announce him to the queen. To give
him his title would offend her; to omit it
would probably offend the king, and the king
was dying. After some delay, at length one
of the king's eldest eunuchs approached him,
saying: 'May it please your majesty, lord
of the universe, protector of the poor, the
infant son of Mulika Ahud has been sent to
pay his respects to your majesty.' 'Let the
sahibalum be admitted,' was the king's order.
'Sahibalum!' echoed the queen, 'Sahibalum!
What king's daughter or what queen's daughter

E

is his mother? What was her dowry? and whence did it come? Bring in the boy.' The infant was brought in. We slaves expected that she would have spat on him, or at the least taken no notice of him. But we were mistaken. Who shall understand the hearts of princes? She was a good and a kind mistress. She spoke kindly to the infant, took him on her knee, and said to him, 'What is your mother doing?' 'She is crying, because my father, the king, is so sick,' was the child's answer. Tears collected in the queen's eyes, she patted the boy's cheek, and kissed him, and the king, who was lying down, took her hand in his, and said to her: 'Begum, his mother is nothing. I give the boy to you. Love him for my sake, when I am gone.' The queen wept, forgave him freely, promised to befriend the boy, but added, ' Why do you talk so? you will soon be well again.' So little idea had she that he was so soon to die!

After the death of Umjid Aly Shah, the frequent and constant *muta* marriages of her son Wajid Aly gave the queen much trouble and annoyance. So far as I am aware, he contracted only one *nikha* (full and complete marriage), and that was with the daughter of his vizier. I speak of the time subsequent to his father's death. He had more than one nikha wife before that, of whom Khash Mehal was chief.

After contracting marriage with his daughter, Wajid Aly was very intimate with the vizier, often allowing him a seat on his own carpet at durbar, contrary to custom, and contrary to the remonstrances of the queen my mistress. This familiarity of the king with her husband, caused the wife of the vizier to assume an importance and dignity of demeanour to which she was not entitled either by position or birth.

I remember, on one occasion, the wife of the vizier called on the queen my mistress at an hour earlier than visitors were usually admitted. It so happened that the queen was up and dressed, but, as she was very tenacious of her dignity, and would not allow anyone to infringe upon it, she sent word to the vizier's wife that, as the usual reception hour had not arrived, she must wait. The visitor was annoyed at this, and said loudly, 'Am I not mother of a queen? Is not my daughter married to the king? If half the power of the state is hers, do I not share in the other half?' The servants, of course, explained that they were only obeying orders. At the usual hour, the vizier's wife was introduced, and the queen received her with great dignity. The vizier's wife, after the usual ceremonies, complained of the queen's servants, and my mistress answered that they had received their orders from her, and could not be blamed for executing them. It was to be regretted, she added, that the vizier's wife had consented to bandy words with them—they being rude and uneducated. The vizier's wife made no suitable apology, but went away in a huff.

That afternoon the queen saw her son, the king, and explained the matter to him, stating that she would not receive the vizier's wife again unless she made a proper apology for her rudeness. The king sent for his father-in-law, and next day the vizier's wife

came to the queen's durbar, threw herself at
her feet, and begged pardon for her rudeness
in arrogating to herself equality with a princess of the royal house of Delhi, widow and
mother of kings.

CHAPTER V.

BAHARA NISSA.

OF all the attendants of the queen, there was none enjoyed so much of her confidence, or to whom she showed so much favour, as Bahara Nissa. Bahara Nissa, with her father and mother and sister, came from the Punjab, and the whole family were proficients in music and singing. Her father, Kala Baha, usually played the drum or tambourine, whilst the two girls danced, and the mother sang. Both the girls were tall, slim, light-coloured, and handsome. They were considered highly educated in Lucknow, and their father had taken every pains to render them accomplished. On their journey from the Punjab to Oudh, a man of some property, Hafiz, had attached himself to the party, out of love for Bahara Nissa. But she would never marry

him. Kala Baha probably expected that, in
such a court as that of Wajid Aly Shah,
their accomplishments of singing and dancing
would raise them to the highest pitch of
favour; and he was not mistaken.

When they were introduced at court, the
eldest girl, Rushkee Alum, was married by
the king forthwith, by muta marriage, and
this was the only one of his muta marriages
that the queen my mistress honoured by her
presence. Generally, indeed, when she saw
all her son's wives drawn up to receive
her, as they sometimes were—for instance,
at Nowa Roz, on New Year's day—she could
not refrain from laughing to see the congre-
gation of all kinds of women, and walked
on with her handkerchief at her mouth,
receiving their salaams and congratulations.
She was a princess born, and they were
chiefly women of no rank by birth.

When Rushkee Alum was thus added to
the number of the king's wives by muta,
Bahara Nissa was taken into the service of
the queen my mistress. The father and
mother of the two girls also got apartments

in the palace, and Bahara Nissa entered into an agreement not to marry for five years. She got a thousand rupees a month from the queen for her attendance, besides rich and valuable presents on all festive occasions. It was not usual for the queen to take up thus with dancing or singing girls, or with strangers of any kind, and therefore, Bahara Nissa's case being so exceptional, she had all the more influence in consequence. The queen trusted her in every matter, and her good sense and prudence, for two years at least, justified this confidence.

At the end of about two years, however, it so happened that a ranee, widow of a rajah from Nanpara, in the Baraitch district, came to court to prefer some complaint of oppression to the queen, accompanied by her brother-in-law, the late rajah's younger brother. The young man's name was Pearee Sahib, and he was tall and good-looking, and of a light colour. Bahara Nissa saw him in the courtyard more than once, and was smitten with love for him. What! can we conquer our own hearts? Of course, she knew it was contrary to her agreement—she was endangering all her court favour, everything, and yet she persevered. She sent a message to him, to say she loved him. He came by stealth. She danced and sang for him, and he was captivated; and they bribed a moollah to marry them. They were married thus privately, and the queen was ignorant of it, and but few of the household even were aware of it. Notwithstanding all the remonstrances of her family, Pearee Sahib lived near the palace, and Bahara Nissa saw him constantly by stealth. He was her lawful husband. She had never been married before.

It was about three or four months after this marriage that Hafiz, the Mussulman gentleman who had followed Bahara Nissa in the vain hope of marrying her, took very ill, and died. He sent the most pressing messages to her, asking her to visit him once during his illness before he died; but she would not. He wrote to the queen, and the queen gave her permission to go; but she was obstinate, and would not. Perhaps she feared poison or assassination at his hands, on account of her marriage. How can I tell? But I do not believe he knew anything of her marriage. At all events, after eight or nine days' constant suffering, and always calling upon her name, he died, alone and unfriended by her, for whom he had sacrificed his family, his country, and his wealth.

Bahara Nissa was now likely to become a mother, and feared exceedingly lest the queen should become aware of it, and of the cause, her secret marriage. Days and nights of anxiety and of alarm did Bahara Nissa pass, pondering over what would be her probable fate—for the punishments in a court are severe. At length, she resolved to take medicines, and to produce miscarriage. The queen saw that her favourite was changed, and that gloom and unhappiness were taking the place of her former life, spirits, and gaiety; but the cause was unknown and unsuspected. At length, Bahara Nissa was confined to her chamber, in great suffering, and unable to continue her attendance. The queen

questioned her servants, and one of her old
faithful slaves, thinking that Bahara Nissa's
career at court was now at an end, told the
whole story. At first the queen would not
believe it; but when the facts were repeated
again and again, she took one of her oldest
and most confidential nurses with her, and
went direct to Bahara Nissa's chamber.
There, of course, she soon discovered the
truth of the statement she had heard, and
she returned, vexed and angry, to her own
apartment.

And now behold how good and kind a
mistress our queen was! Another queen
would have had both Bahara Nissa and her
husband impaled upon red-hot iron stakes,
or taken some other vengeance equally signal,
for was not punishment well merited by
both of them? But our queen was not such.
She simply put Pearee Sahib into prison,
and banished Bahara Nissa from her presence, giving her, however, an ample allow-
ance, and sending word to her that the crime
she had committed in destroying her infant
was greater than in breaking her engagement.

Bahara Nissa was long ill. Her life was in danger. Her sister exerted herself in behalf of Pearee Sahib, and he was released after three days. On her recovery, Bahara Nissa came often to pay her respects to the queen, but for a long time she was not admitted, nor were her letters and petitions answered. But the queen's heart was soft, and in a few months she relented, and Bahara Nissa was restored to place and favour.

Years rolled on, and there were rumours that all was not right. It was said the English were very angry with the king, who spent all his time in dancing and singing and fiddling—sometimes in female, sometimes in male attire, surrounded by his wives and eunuchs. The queen my mistress often remonstrated with him, and cried bitterly over his follies and his inattention to her remonstrances. But it was of no avail. Bahara Nissa was a faithful attendant to her, and was faithful also to her husband—a rare thing in a dancing girl.

At length the catastrophe came. One

morning the queen was dressing after her
bath, everything as usual, when a large
sealed letter was brought in to her. The
messenger said it was from the vizier, and
was most important. The queen read
Persian like a moonshi, and immediately,
half-dressed as she was, opened the letter
and read it. I was preparing the hookah in
the same room. I saw the letter opened.
I saw the queen's face turning paler and
paler as she read it. At length, holding the
letter in her hands, and without stopping to
put on her shoes, she walked rapidly out
into the courtyard, exclaiming, 'The kingdom
is destroyed!' It was in the Dowlut Khana,
and the courtyard alone separated us from
the king's apartments. Thither went the
queen, bareheaded and barefooted, hastily.
Several of us followed; one with a muslin
sheet or veil, another with the shoes, another
with an umbrella. She pushed us aside as
we offered one thing and another. ' No, no,'
said she, ' I must do without attendance, as
I must do without a throne—perhaps without a home or food—in my old age.' And

the queen wept as she went, and Bahara Nissa wept as she followed, and we all went after them, and lamented with beating of breasts, although we knew not for certain what calamity had happened.

The queen walked without ceremony or announcement straight into the room where the king her son was sitting. None hindered her, all made way for her, wondering and in silence.

The king was sitting alone and crying. When he saw his mother the queen enter, he covered his face with his hands, and sobbed aloud. She made him three salaams as she advanced, saying, 'Are you now satisfied? Have you got at last the wages of your dancing, your singing, and your fiddling? Have I not often told you it would come to this? . Did any of your fathers sing and dance and fiddle in women's clothes?' Bahara Nissa alone ventured to remonstrate with the queen. The king said never a word.

After some little expostulation on the part of Bahara Nissa, the queen ceased her reproaches, and said, 'It is true. All this is too late now; leave us alone.' We all turned and went out, and the queen alone remained with her son, taking her muslin veil as we departed. About two or three o'clock in the afternoon, the English resident came, and there was another long conference, at which the queen was present. In the evening soldiers came into Lucknow from the cantonments, and the cannon were removed from the palaces, and we knew that the king's reign was at an end, and that the English raj had begun.

It was at this trying time that Bahara Nissa greatly comforted the queen by her counsels and her sympathy. She was an invaluable attendant, always calm, self-possessed, and prudent.

The great men of the kingdom came to offer troops and munitions of war to fight against the English, but the king refused. They then came to the queen my mistress, and she took a night to think over it; and next morning, as Bahara Nissa had advised, she also said 'No.' That very day the queen announced her intention of going to England to us all. 'I will go,' said she, 'to the English queen. She is also the mother of a son, and I will ask her not to take my son's crown from him. Has she not crowns and kingdoms and wealth enough? Must all the world belong to one?' 'How shall *you* go?' said we; '*you* that fear a river so much —how shall you go, and cross the great black water, the boundless sea?' But she would not listen to us, and Bahara Nissa began to prepare for the journey, for Bahara Nissa had said she would take her husband with her, and go with the queen to England. The king went to Calcutta a fortnight afterwards, and was no more a king, except in name.

One of the preparations for the journey consisted in the construction of a large brick chamber, built under a reservoir of water in the palace, for the reception of jewels, gold and silver furniture of all kinds, and other treasure which the queen did not want to take with her to England. The water was drained off. An underground compartment was constructed, and the valuables were

placed in it, covered with matting and oiled
cloth, or wax-cloth. A flat brick roof supported on beams was then built, and this roof
was the bottom of the tank or reservoir.
The water was let in, and all appeared to be
as before. It is said that several lacs' worth
(or tens of thousands of pounds' worth) of
property was deposited in that chamber, and
so secretly was the work done, that only a
few even of our household knew of it. Bahara Nissa trusted and befriended me, and I
knew it.

At length all things were ready for the
journey to England, and the queen, with
some of her attendants, Bahara Nissa and
myself amongst the number, started for Calcutta. All the rest of the household had
been discharged or pensioned off.

The queen took water enough with her on
starting from Lucknow to supply her till her
arrival in Calcutta. Why she should have
done so, I don't know. There did not appear
to be any want of water on the road.

Bahara Nissa took her husband with her
to England; and on the queen's death, made

F

the pilgrimage with him to Mecca, before returning to Lucknow. Gholam Hussain, my husband, accompanied me. Arrived safely in Calcutta, the queen my mistress resolved to visit her son's chief wife, Khash Mehal, and to depart in friendship with all. There had been no communication between them since the attempt to poison the hookah, formerly described. The queen was living with the ex-king in Calcutta, and, in pursuance of her plan of being at enmity with none before her departure, went one day unannounced into Khash Mehal's apartment. Khash Mehal saw her enter, got up quickly, and left the room. The queen then turned to Bahara Nissa, and said, 'Here am I, the head and the elder, stooping to effect a reconciliation with my daughter-in-law, whom I have never injured, and my face is blackened, I am treated with contempt.' Bahara Nissa went to the attendants of Khash Mehal, got her own sister also to use her influence; and just as the queen my mistress was turning to depart, Khash Mehal came into the apartment, threw herself on the queen's neck, and embraced her. Thus happily was a reunion effected before the queen's final departure to Europe where she died.

Bitterly, very bitterly, did the queen weep the day she took leave of her son, the ex-king and his children, to go on board the steamer that was to carry her off. Bahara Nissa accompanied her, and managed everything for her. She was always wise and prudent. Evil luck was there, however; for, as the goods were being handed into the steamer, one box of ornaments dropped into the water and was lost. We all regarded it as an evil omen, and the queen, as we all know, never returned. Her son the general went with her.

On the death of the queen in Europe, Bahara Nissa returned to Lucknow, and lived with her husband Pearee Sahib. She is living there now. They are both alive, and although her beauty is not now what it once was, yet her form is still elegant, her black hair is rich and lustrous, and three feet long, and her husband loves her. Children! no, she has no children. That is the punishment of her crime, just as my being childless is

my evil fate, in that I eat up my mother's life
at my birth.   God's will be done.   I take a
little opium, and am content.

There is no more to be said of Bahara
Nissa : but what of the treasure that was
buried under the cistern? you ask.   It is a
long story.   When I returned to Lucknow,
with my husband, he resumed his shop near
the palace.   But the English began knock-
ing down bazaars and planting grass every-
where, and, amongst the rest, our bazaar
was swept away.   We lived for some time
on the jewels and ornaments I had collected
in the queen's service, and we were both
getting poorer when, just before the mutiny
broke out, one of the queen's muta wives
then in Lucknow, mother of a son, Brijis
Kudr by name, asked me to live with her.
I went, and, when the mutiny broke out a
few months after, the sepoys came and took
Brijis Kudr to make him king in the room
of his father in Calcutta.   He was but a
child, and his mother was very averse to his

being made king, for she knew herself, and
many told her, it would not be for long, and
that when the English caught him, they
would hang him. She threw herself at the
feet of the sepoy officer who came to take
her son to the great mosque to be crowned,
and cried out, 'He is my only son—spare
him—he is not the rightful heir—you know
he is not—do not make him king—between
you and the English he will be sure to be
killed.' But some people's hearts are hard
as grinding-stones, and the sepoys' hearts
were not soft. They took him, and made
him king, and his mother was treated with
royal state, but she knew it was all mockery,
and but for a short time, and her heart was
sad.

How she came to hear of the treasure
that the queen my mistress had buried, I
do not know. But she did hear of it, and
wanted me to point out where it was. She
knew that silver bedsteads, stools, cups,
plates, and golden ornaments were all hidden
somewhere, and I was importuned about it.
But I would rather have been torn asunder

by wild horses than betray my mistress's secret. All that she could say, all that her attendants could say, would not drag the secret from me; and seeing that she was getting angry about it, I left her service and fled to my native village. I found no rest there. I was a sheeah, an outcast, and I had no friends. At length, after much wandering, I returned to Lucknow, and the first news I heard from my husband, on finding him again, was that some one else had informed Brijis Kudr's mother where the treasure was, and she had found it. I went to the place by stealth, and found it even so. The cistern was dry, the bottom of it torn up, the secret chamber half filled with rubbish, and all the treasure gone.

Yes! for two or three years after the mutiny we lived very well, I and my husband. We were well off. He was successful in business. But then everything went wrong, and I became a servant to English ladies. My mistress is very good, but I shall never get such a mistress as the queen again.

CHAPTER VI.

Nowa Roz, or New Year's day, was a time
of family reunion and feasting in the palace,
as it is amongst poorer Mussulmans. I can
remember, when a child at home, before I
was carried off to Lucknow, that on New
Year's day we got new dresses, and that we
sprinkled each other with a red fluid made by
boiling down the flower called *har·singal*,
and that all the family met together for
feasting and congratulations and giving of
presents. The beginning of the New Year
was considered a fit time, the fittest time, for
mirth and fun and jollity.

Now it was exactly the same at the palace,
only that, of course, everything was done in a
more formal way ; and everything was rich
and splendid, not poor and dirty and squalid
as in the villages.

The king always paid his mother, the queen my mistress, the compliment to come to her early on New Year's day, with Khash Mehal, his chief wife, and her son the heir apparent, to offer nuzzers or presents, and to wish her health, prosperity, and long life. On that day the queen put on her bravest apparel, and was loaded with jewellery. All her household took a pride in seeing her look her best, and wearing her richest clothing and ornaments; and throughout the year, it was often on New Year's day only that she would consent to be thus decked out.

When the king and Khash Mehal and the heir apparent had presented their gifts, then came a troop of the king's wives, a hundred or a hundred and twenty of them, whom the queen would not receive at other times. Some of them were mere children, many of them very pretty, some old, one was a negress, but all came trooping in in their best clothes, to the great amusement of the queen, who never looked upon them all without laughing.

Then came the general, with his eldest son and one or two of his wives; but those .

whom he considered pretty, or whom he
valued, the general never brought, lest his
brother the king should see them and take
them to himself. All came with gifts.

Great pitchers of red dye stood ready for
use in the verandahs, and the queen sprinkled
a little, a very little, on each, and was in
turn sprinkled by them. Sweetmeats were
then handed round, and the morning's amusements wound up with the servants trooping
into the courtyard, and plentifully daubing
each other over with the dye, which was done
with much mirth and laughter.

Fans, large and small, to be used by the
hand, were prepared for this day, and were
neatly trimmed with red cloth, and handed
from one to the other, with a slight waving,
as if to fan the party to whom each fan was
offered.

Such were the morning's amusements—
such, combined with music and dancing and
singing, which were never wanting in the
palace on occasions of mirth and festivity.
But it was in the evening that the greatest
hilarity prevailed. For two or three hours

in the afternoon the queen usually lay down, fatigued with the morning's ceremony, but she never lay down without first reading prayers from the Koran, so zealous in religious matters was she.

The longest room in the palace was the scene of festivity in the evening, and in this preparation was made for the family banquet. New carpets were spread, and over them two long cloths from end to end, on each side of which plates were arranged. At right angles to this, across the top of the room, was another cloth, supported by a carpet of the richest material, fringed with gold lace. The most splendid cushions were here made ready, and massive gold and silver articles displayed on all sides. At this shorter tablecloth, the seat of honour, at the upper end of the room, the queen my mistress, and the king, and Khash Mehal, and the heir apparent, and the general and his eldest son, took their places, amid the loud flourish of trumpets, the playing of bands, and the roar of cannon.

The chandeliers from the roof were all lit

up, and the wall-shades by the sides of the
large mirrors on the walls ; the room was a
blaze of light, and the sparkling of gold and
silver cups, and plates, and jewellery, and
rich dresses, reflected back by the large
mirrors, made a gorgeous scene. It was as
the court of Indra, the palace of the Peris.
Then came the other wives of the king,
trooping in, to take their places—some tall,
some short, dark and fair, young and old,
beautiful and ugly, all in rich kinkobs and
cloths of gold, wearing their finest jewellery,
and soft silvery voices rang forth in laughter,
and the sweet tones of girlhood were mingled
with the roar of drums and trumpets and
all kinds of musical instruments without. The
English are a great people, and do mighty
wonders, but they have no assemblies like
that so rich and gorgeous and splendid.
Down the whole length of the room the
chandeliers flashed upon rich garments and
gems, and many beautiful faces, all reflected
in the mirrors around; and as the music without ceased, and the banquet began, the hum
of many voices rose from the long lines of

sitting figures, subdued voices, and whispering intermingled with the soft laugh of girlhood, and happiness was over all.

And I, did I not see it? Was I not every year in the room? Who gave the queen her hookah, but I? and who could once see that beautiful scene, and fail to remember it for ever after?

When the banquet was concluded, music and singing and dancing filled up the hours till near midnight—no entertainment lasted over midnight. In that, as in so many other things, the feasts and festivals of the court were unlike the rejoicings and parties of the sahibs. Have I not seen the balls and parties of the English sahibs and ladies continue till the morning? It was never so at court.

Two years before annexation, the queen my mistress was not on good terms with the king her son. I do not know what was the cause of difference. Doubtless it was connected with some affairs of state. I was but a slave who prepared the hookah : what could I know of it? However, this I know, that on that occasion the king did not come as

usual with Khash Mehal and his eldest son,
the heir apparent, to pay the usual morning
visit, with presents, and the queen was sad,
but said nothing. In the evening all was as
usual. The general, who loved the queen his
mother, and was beloved by her, had come,
as was the custom ; and, on the next New
Year's day the general came early to his
mother's court to present his gifts, and to
offer his congratulations, and stopped with
her, not going, as was his wont, to visit the
king also. The king noticed the absence of
the general, and asked about it, and they
told him, ' He is with the queen his mother.'
The king waited for him to come all day, but
finding he did not, and fearing that some
family intrigue might be formed against him,
for the English were daily threatening—so it
is said, at least—he came towards evening to
pay his usual visit to his mother.

The queen had been lying down, and when
she heard he was come, she went and lay
down again, and ordered her attendants to
tell the king she was lying down as usual, and
would not be disturbed. He waited some

time, and then went away, and we hastened to tell the queen. On hearing this, she arose But the king had only gone round, and entered her apartments by another way, and before any news could be brought, himself entered the room where she was, the female guards not daring to prevent him. ' Did you not tell me his majesty had gone ? ' she asked of her attendants on seeing him, and for some time she refused to speak to him, or to receive his present. But at length she relented, and conversed amicably with him, and all was as usual, except that she would not recognise or acknowledge Khash Mehal at all.

On the last New Year's day before annexation, the king came with his eldest son so early that the queen was not ready to receive him, and he was kept waiting a short time. She certainly had great weight in the kingdom, and was highly esteemed both by the English resident and by the nobility for her virtue, prudence, and wisdom. Perhaps it was on this account the king strove so much not to offend her.

CHAPTER VII.

MINOR RELIGIOUS FESTIVALS AND FASTS.

THE fast of the Ramazan was rigidly kept at the palace. For thirty days, sometimes in the hottest months of the year, nothing was allowed to be eaten or drunk from sunrise to sunset. Women who are in the family-way, and who are nursing, are exempted from this rigorous abstinence in the Koran, but no exceptions were made in the queen's court. Nor meat, nor drink, nor the hookah, was permitted for those thirty days, from sunrise to sunset. As soon as it was proclaimed from the minarets that the sun was down, the long day's fast was first broken by a pinch of salt, and then a long draught of water, or sherbet, or some cooling drink, previously prepared, was brought in and partaken of. Eating, drinking, and prayers filled up the night, for we all slept as much as possible in the day, to get over the long day's fast as pleasantly as possible.

On the first appearance of the moon after the fast of the Ramazan, the feast of the Ede commenced. It is a day of joy and visiting of friends, and mutual congratulations. New clothes are worn and gifts are given and received. At the great musjid we had a grand service at nine o'clock in the morning on the Ede day, to which the queen always went, and returned home to partake plentifully and joyfully of the favourite dish of the season, *semay* (a kind of vermicelli), which was boiled in milk, with dates, pistachio nuts, and spices to flavour it—an excellent dish when properly prepared. The queen always warned us on the morning of the Ede to abstain from angry words, disputes, and quarrelling during the whole of that day. On that day especially all should be peace and harmony and thankfulness. The children too got presents of toys on the Ede, and in the evening the gardens were lit up, and, with fruit and flowers and music and dancing and singing, the hardships of the Ramazan were forgotten.

The Bukra Ede (Ede of the goat), celebrated some days after the Ede, is in remembrance of Abraham having been about to
sacrifice his son Ishmael, when the angel
stopped him, and threw down a goat from
heaven for him to sacrifice instead. It was
not his son Isaac he was going to sacrifice,
but Ishmael—is it not all written in the
Koran? Well, when the goat fell, it so happened that it fell on a fish and a locust, and
killed them both; and hence a fish and a
locust are the only two animals a good Mussulman can eat, without having them first
killed by cutting their throats. The queen
used to explain all these things to us, as
we waited on her. She was learned as a
moollah.

On the Bukra Ede every good Mussulman must eat the flesh of a goat, if he
wishes to get into Paradise. The queen libe-
rally supplied us with goat's flesh on the
Bukra Ede, and besides that had two camels
killed, so that every servant of the household
might get a small portion of camel's flesh to
eat. Those who sacrifice and eat camels on

G

the Bukra Ede will enter Paradise riding on a camel, whilst other good and true believers will only enter it on a goat. Now, the advantage of riding the camel is, that from the trees of Paradise the riders on the camel can pluck the luscious fruit as they go along, whilst those riding on the goat cannot reach it. All this, and more of religious knowledge, did we learn from our good mistress the queen, who was learned and pious.

The Subrath is a feast of woe, in honour of the dead. Flour, ghee or clarified butter, sugar, almonds, and raisins, are all made into a kind of paste, called *hulwa*. When all is ready, and cakes of unleavened bread baked, a space is cleared for the ceremony, and a pan with fire in it placed in the midst. Five unleavened cakes are placed in the cleared space round the fire. The family dead are then enumerated one by one, name by name, and as each name is mentioned a portion of the cake and of the hulwa is dropped into the fire, and good wishes for his condition in the future life are expressed. All the family dead for two generations back were thus named in the queen's household, but it is not right on these occasions to mention those who have died within two moons of the Subrath. If five or six moons have elapsed, then the names may be mentioned; and it being the first mention of them, a longer address is made use of, and more ceremony used in naming the name of the deceased. The ceremony is then concluded by pouring out forty jars of water. Forty is a sacred number, the queen explained to us— many events being recorded in the Koran with forty attached—forty days, forty years, forty prophets, forty stars, and such like. The rich add to this giving of alms to the poor, and in the doing of this our queen was very liberal, and we servants had our little advantages in it. Lastly lamps are lit upon the graves of the deceased, which makes the Subrath of the Mussulmans look like the Dewalee of the Hindus. But they are very different. Are not the Hindus pagans and worshippers of idols and unbelievers?

CHAPTER VIII.

THE MOHURRIM.

THE MOHURRIM is a time of mourning kept in remembrance of the deaths of Hassain and Hoossen, the sons of Huzrut Aly.* The Soonnies only celebrate the Mohurrim for ten days, and they carry about no images or models. The Sheeahs celebrate the festival for forty days, with much parade, and images, and models, and some acting. During this fast, or festival of woe, no tobacco or pawn (betel-nut chewed with spices and lime) is used, and men and women are not to indulge in any sensual pleasures, but all ought to mourn and lament, with soul and body. The queen kept the Mohurrim so strictly,

---

* The term *Huzrut* is equivalent to our *Saint.* Noah and Abraham and Christ are always spoken of by Mussulmans as Huzrut Noah, &c.

that she would not change her clothes those forty days, used no oil or sweet scents, put no *missee* (tooth-powder) to her teeth, nor *mayndee* (colouring matter like rouge) to her hands or feet, and left off all her ornaments. No marriages ought to be celebrated or contracted during the Mohurrim, and in properly conducted households the men and women live separately at that time.

Every Mohurrim the queen instructed us diligently in the story of the deaths of Hassain and Hoossen, and I heard it all so often that I remember every word of it. The queen would tell it thus :—

Shortly after the time of the Prophet, whose name be always blessed, there were four brothers, leaders of the faithful : their names were Huzrut Aly, Yahudy, Zenabia Abas Alaam, and Zenabia Ameen Alaam. They disagreed amongst themselves on points of faith, too difficult for servants to understand ; Abas Alaam sided with Huzrut Aly, who was the true follower of the Prophet, and Ameen Alaam sided with Yahudy, who was a father of error. The commander-in-chief of Huzrut Aly's forces was Syud Salár, who, after a little, deserted, with all his forces, to Yahudy, and a civil war began. Cursed be those that breed dissension amongst the faithful! In the course of the war Yahudy, whose name and memory be for ever defiled, bribed one of the bodyguard of Huzrut Aly to cut off his chief's head, and the bribe was his daughter in marriage, the betrothed of Hassain, son of Huzrut Aly. This girl was beautiful as a houri, and the bribe was more than enough to corrupt even a good man. But so attached and devoted were the few followers of the saint, that the one who was faithless waited long in vain for an opportunity to execute his wicked purpose, born of the devil. The army of Yahudy was large, and Huzrut Aly, with only a few followers, was shut up, besieged, and in want of all things—water and provisions and ammunition.

At length the day of the martyrdom of the saint dawned. As he was on his way to the musjid for morning prayers, according to his wont, a goose caught hold of his robe, and would have prevented his going. He laughed only, and said, ' I know my enemy is waiting for me.' A little further on, a goat would have impeded him, but he gave the same answer, and went on his way. From that day the goose and the goat are animals esteemed by all good Sheeahs as sacred. As the saint entered the musjid, the traitor, who had been bribed, was standing behind the door hidden, and lifted his sword unseen of all but God and the saint. ' Strike,' said the saint, ' I fear not.' The weapon fell from the hand of the traitor, and the saint passed on. But the devil gives strength to his own, and the traitor watched the saint, and when he was bowing his head in earnest prayer, the traitor—may curses light on him and all his posterity!—cut off the saint's head with one blow, and escaped. The two sons of the saint, Hassain and Hoossen, aided by God, carried on the war. And now the camp of the faithful was suffering dreadfully from want of water. One of the four daughters of Huzrut Aly was in the camp, beautiful as a peri, and she too was in torture for want of water. Her uncle Abas Alaam loved her, saw her sufferings, and, taking a skin for water, cut his way through the enemy to a well, and filled the skin with water, though exposed to the fire of an army. As he was carrying off the skin full of water, he was wounded in the shoulder, and his arm was disabled, and the skin of water fell to the ground. . He seized it then with his teeth, and was wounded again as he carried it along. The enemy fired their arrows at the skin to let the water out, and when he arrived where his niece was, there was but enough to quench her thirst, and he laid down and died.

In the meantime the body of Huzrut Aly lay for a whole month undecayed in the musjid, which was at a considerable distance from the quarters of the faithful. Hassain and Hoossen determined to set out to bring in their father's body. All their female relations dissuaded them with many tears, saying, 'You too will be killed;' but they felt no fear, and prepared their horses, and a mule to carry the body, and set out fully armed. Arrived at the musjid, they found a tiger guarding the body. They lifted the corpse, put it on the mule's back, and no sooner got outside the musjid, than they were furiously attacked. Holding the string of the led mule, they fought their way back, but the string was cut, and the mule went off with the body, and they fainting and wounded got back alive.

Soon after in a great battle the forces of the faithful were routed by the enemy, on whose heads be shame; and the two sons and the brother of Huzrut Aly were killed in the fight. Notice was brought to Lady Fatima, the widow of the saint, and she and her four daughters, weeping and barefooted, throwing ashes on their heads, went forth to seek for the dead. After long search in vain, they took refuge, tired and weary, in a tent.

And now behold the perfidy of slaves! Whoso trusteth in a slave will be certain to be betrayed, and the Prophet saith likewise. A slave of the saint saw them there, and, anxious to gain the favour of Yahudy, tore their veils from them, and turned them out of the tent with blows, and thus, with exposed faces, and barefooted, went forth the weeping widow and daughters of the saint, with none to help them—a piteous case!

Weeping and lamenting, they wandered forth on the battle-field, and their great enemy Yahudy saw them, recognised them, and, smiling, left them to their fate. Hard as adamant the heart of the wicked! But faithless as slaves are and will be, yet now a slave befriended them ; showing that, even amongst the worst of mankind, there are some good. This slave conducted them to a forest, where they might lie concealed, and Fatima spun, and her daughters ground corn, and thus they supported themselves, in retirement, ungazed upon by man. They had no veils, but Fatima and her daughters collected in the forest 180 pieces of rags, and, having washed them, made a sheet for a veil, which they wore in turn when they went out. Perseverance and trust in God will overcome all evils.

Things continued thus for a month or so, when a wicked band of the enemy, children of the devil, found them out, and murdered them all without pity, mercy, or remorse.

Such was the story of Hassain and Hoossen, as the queen told it to us, weeping as she told it, and we never heard it without loud lamentations and beating of breasts, and tears. A representation of the tomb of the martyrs, called the *tazia*, is carried in procession at the end of the Mohurrim, and buried.

In the palace, tazias of rich materials were always kept in some of the largest apartments, and carried about in procession at the Mohurrim. During the lifetime of Umjid Aly Shah there were only two of these tazias of silver, each with its silver altar before it ; but in the reign of Wajid Aly there were nine of them, and they were kept in the silver *baradhurry* in the palace. The silver altars were covered with a black cloth, at the time of the Mohurrim, and on these altars votive offerings called *alums*, silver hands in shape, and daggers and swords and such-like, were displayed to view.

On the floor between the tazias curiously shaped coloured lanterns were placed, with scented wax candles in them, which were lit at night. During the entire forty days the baradhurry was brilliantly illuminated every night, but on the ninth night the light was as that of day.

On the seventh day a procession took place in honour of Kassim, the cousin of Hassain, who lost his life on his wedding-day, and trays of silver covered with the leaves of the mayndee are carried about then from house to house, with weeping and lamentation. The mayndee yields the red dye and paint so much used in marriage feasts and processions, and hence the trays of mayndee carried about in memory of Kassim's untimely death.

On the eighth day ceremonies are performed in honour of Abas Alaam, who so bravely brought the water for his favourite niece.

But the ninth is the great day of the fast. In the mosques there is then a continuous reading of the Koran all day long, kept up by successive relays of moollahs, and the lives and deaths of Huzrut Aly and his martyred family are related; and on that night the illumination in the palace and the bazaars and the city was as if all the stars of heaven

had come down into Lucknow. The tazias
were carried about in procession, and a horse
—the horse of Hassain, called Dhool-dhool—
all stuck over with arrows, followed the tazias,
and the weeping women, with loud lamentations and beating of breasts, followed, and
the multitude took up the wail, and the city
mourned.

In the queen's household we had recita-
tions all night on that ninth night ; for the
queen was devout. None slept. The martyrdom of Huzrut Aly and his family was
described again and again, and prints of the
chief scenes in the saint's life were exhibited,
and we all wept and wailed all night long. I
remember particularly the pictures of Fatima
and her daughters, without veils and barefooted, the hut in the forest, and the spinning-
wheel, and the sheet of the 180 rags, and last
of all the horrid murder. Oh ! it was a sad
sight. Three times during the night a solemn
farewell to the dead brothers was spoken, the
last farewell just as day dawned.

On the morning of the day when all the
tazias, except the silver ones, were buried,

they were ranged in one of the courtyards
of the palace, and three hundred men, reciters
of the woes of the saint's martyrdom, and
the martyrdom of his family, were engaged,
and other men rattled together bits of wood
as the people lamented. The men and women
struck their breasts at intervals, shouting 'Hassain!' and ' Hoossen!' and it was no
uncommon thing for blood to flow from this
striking of the breasts, and serious injury to
be done. On the conclusion of the recitation,
the queen my mistress and the king and all
the royal family walked in procession round
the tazias, three times. They then threw
dust and chopped-up straw into the air, in
imitation of the ashes Fatima and her daughters had strewn on their heads, and then all
of them uncovered their heads, and beat their
breasts, shouting ' Hassain! Hoossen!' just
as the servants and the multitude did. The
farewell benediction was always spoken first
by the queen my mistress, and afterwards by
the king.

This done, the procession for the burial of
the tazias was formed. Bearers of alums or

votive offerings first, then readers and reciters, then mourners, then more alum-bearers, and so on, till the tazias themselves came; the readers and reciters and mourners with each. The tazias were usually composed of a framework of wood, covered with silk, and the sides of talc or glass—all of the shape of the tomb, decorated with flags and such like, of brilliant colours, with tinsel representations of the water-skin of Abas Alaam, the spinning-wheel of Fatima, and other memorable objects connected with this mournful history.

When the procession had gone ahead some forty yards or so, the royal family followed with uncovered heads—my mistress first. Again they all beat their breasts, and cried 'Hassain! Hoossen!' and lamented. They went so for about half a mile of enclosed walks, not in the public roads, and then returned, in their conveyance, to spend the day in reading, and praying, and in religious exercises. At least, so the queen spent it. No one was allowed to eat a morsel of food, or to drink a drop of water, all that day, till the procession returned from the burial of the tazias, which was about sunset. Even the sucking infant on that day was deprived of its food till the burial was over, so strict was the fast.

But rigorous as the fast really is, it is not called a fast, and two or three grains of salt are put on the tongue in the morning, to prevent its being a fast, because it is said that the wife of the traitor who slew Huzrut Aly fasted for joy at the success of her husband's treason. May her tomb be defiled!

During the first five days of the Mohurrim, meat and drink were distributed to the poor, and on the sixth and seventh days large quantities of excellent and savoury dishes were given away—kabobs, and pillaus, and khoormas. On the eighth day the breakfast of Abas Alaam is offered, but only those who are pure in mind and body, having bathed and put on clean clothes, dare to partake of it. Even mentioning his name with unwashed mouth is a sin which has been severely punished. On the afternoon of the eighth day sherbet is given to the poor in memory of Hassain, and on the ninth day they get a preparation of rice and milk, boiled together, and called *khere*.

The temple of Abas Alaam is crowded with suppliants during the first ten days of the Mohurrim. He is supposed to be beneficent to all who worship in sincerity and purity. He grants cures of diseases, children, and release from trouble and sorrow. If any particular object be prayed for, such as a child, a figure of it is offered. The figure first offered is of little or no value, but if the gift is granted, then a figure of silver is given. These offerings are made during the Mohurrim, and after it is over the priests take what they require for themselves, and dispose of the rest for the benefit of the poor.

I know of many who got children by prayers to Abas Alaam. The queen's daughter, whose marriage was not a happy one, had been married some years without children. She made a votive offering of a boy in silver, and before next Mohurrim she had a son. No, he is not alive now. He died eighteen months after. She is childless now. Such is fate.

H

The last Mohurrim, before the English rule, was in 1855, and everyone that was there must remember how many signs there were of coming misfortune. The horse of Huzrut Aly, called Dhool-dhool, which comes in apparently stuck with arrows, when introduced into the baradhurry to go seven times round the tazias, destroyed the carpet. This was one omen. Again, two of the chandeliers in the palace fell, with a great crash, on the ninth day, and all of us said to ourselves and to each other, 'What does this portend?' Was not that another bad omen? And one of the tazias took fire, and was burned up. Was not that another bad omen? Last of all, a great comet appeared in the sky, the point of which was turned towards Oudh, and the tail towards Mecca, and the wise knew that it was for the rising and falling of kingdoms.

It was the custom of the king, Wajid Aly, to have two figures made during the Mohurrim—one of Yahudy, and one of Syud Salár ; and he had the faces of the figures blackened, and a chain of old shoes hung round

their necks in contempt, and two *mehters*, or
sweepers (men of the lowest caste), stood on
each side with their sweeping brooms in
their hands instead of the usual handsome
attendants with chowries to brush away the
flies. And the king shot at these figures with
arrows, and struck them with a sword, and
exposed them to every indignity, decent and
indecent, and his companions did the same
when the king was tired; and last of all the
two figures were burnt with fire, and their
ashes were scattered to the winds of heaven.
It was thus that the king displayed his zeal
for the faith; but God was not pleased with
him, or surely he would never have lost his
kingdom. So said the queen my mistress
often, and she was wise.

CHAPTER IX.

LADY FATIMA.

IT was some time, perhaps three or four years, before the English annexation, when the queen had been annoyed and inconvenienced by exhibitions of pride and want of attention on the part of some of her chief attendants, that she called her female household together, and related to them the story of Huzrut Fatima. I heard it several times afterwards, and it is all fixed in my memory, so that I can tell it nearly word for word : —

Lady Fatima was wife of Huzrut Aly, and mother of Hassain and Hoossen ; and whilst she and her husband lived happily and in great splendour together, a poor grass-cutter and his wife lived at no great distance from their palace. Now, the Lady Fatima was proud, and did not wait upon and tend her

husband with all that assiduity that a wife
ought : this was her only fault.

One day Huzrut Aly said to her, ' Beebee
Fatima, that poor grass-cutter's wife will
enter heaven before you.' ' Before me ?' said
the Lady Fatima haughtily. ' How can that
be, when I am the wife of a prophet ? ' And
the saint answered, ' Nevertheless, what I say
is true ; for she will hold the bridle of the
camel on which you enter Paradise, and set
her foot in it before you.' ' And why should
that be so ? ' asked the lady. ' See her, and
judge for yourself,' was the saint's answer.

So the next morning the Lady Fatima went
herself to the grass-cutter's cottage, and
knocked at the door. ' Who's there ? ' asked
the grass-cutter's wife from within. ' It is I,
Huzrut Beebee Fatima,' was the lady's answer.
' And what is it you require, lady ? ' asked
the poor woman, still from within. ' I
want to enter and see you and your cottage,' said the lady. ' I have not enquired
my husband's wishes in this matter,' said the
poor woman. ' He is at his daily work : I
cannot open the door now ; when he returns

I will ask him, and to-morrow I will tell you what he says.' Lady Fatima returned home and told Huzrut Aly all that had taken place. His reply was, ' Persevere, see, and judge.'

Next morning Lady Fatima went out walking with her son Hassain, and called at the grass-cutter's cottage again. She knocked at the door; the same question was asked by the poor woman from within, ' Who's there? ' and the same answer was returned, ' It is I, Huzrut Beebee Fatima.' Just then Hassain, her son, said something; and as the grass-cutter's wife was coming to the door to open it, she heard his voice. ' Is there anyone with you, Lady Fatima?' she asked from within. ' Only my son Hassain,' was the answer. ' I had my husband's permission to open the door for you,' said the poor woman; ' but I did not ask him anything about your son. I cannot open for him also.' So the Lady Fatima returned home, saying she would come again next day. And when she told her husband Huzrut Aly what had taken place, he said again, ' Persevere, see, and judge.'

So the next day the Lady Fatima was walk-

ing out with her two sons, Hassain and
Hoossen, and went to the cottage as before,
and the same dialogue took place ; but when
the poor woman saw that the Lady Fatima
had her two sons with her, she would not
open, saying that she had only permission
from her husband to open to the Lady Fatima
and her son Hassain ; but she would ask her
husband, on his return, if the Lady Fatima
chose to come again. So the Lady Fatima
returned home, and told her husband Huzrut
Aly what had taken place, and got the same
answer, ' Persevere, see, and judge.'

On the grass-cutter coming home in the
evening, his wife told him what she had
done, and, instead of commending her for it,
he exclaimed, ' O miserable woman! do
you want to ruin me by sending away a lady
such as Huzrut Beebee Fatima day by day
from my door? If it is her good pleasure to
come again, throw open the door, whoever
may be with her, and admit her without an
instant's delay.'

So next day, when Lady Fatima and her
two sons came to the cottage, the poor

woman threw open the door, and invited them to enter, before the lady had time to knock. Lady Fatima entered, seated herself, and looked around her. She observed that everything in the cottage was poor; but everything was tidy, neat, and clean. A small fire burned on the floor, and an iron plate, or griddle, was standing by it, ready to bake the thin unleavened bread used by the poor, called *chupatties*, and a vessel of pease was also near. In another place cold food and well-filtered water stood ready. There were two beds ready, one with a pillow and thick counterpane, the other simply a framework covered with tape. A rope was hanging up on the wall, and a cane stood in the corner.

'Tell me, my good woman,' said the lady, 'what are all these things for?' 'All for my husband's comfort, when he returns home tired and weary,' said the woman. 'If he wishes to sleep, here is his bed ready; if he only wishes to rest himself, the other bed, covered with that broad tape, is ready. Warm and cold water are ready for him to wash, and, as to food, cold food is ready in one corner, and he can have warm chupatties and dhall in a few minutes. Behold also his hookah ready. 'And what,' asked the lady, 'is the meaning of this rope and cane?' 'These too,' said the woman, 'are for my husband's comfort and convenience. Should he find cause to be displeased with me, the rope is ready with which he can tie me up, and the cane is ready with which to beat me, without the trouble of searching for them!'

Lady Fatima said nothing in reply, but thought much, and went on her way home.

That same evening Huzrut Aly returned to his apartment, looking flushed and weary, for the day was hot. Lady Fatima took a fan up at once, and began fanning him. They had been married many years, yet she had never done this before, so he saw that the lesson he had wished to teach had been learned by her. He was very glad, so glad that his heart begun to swell with gratitude to God, to such an extent that his whole body was inflamed, and his vest became so tight it threatened to choke him at the neck.

The Almighty saw the danger that threatened his friend the prophet, and, calling the angel Gabriel, said, ' Go down forthwith to Huzrut Aly, and say to him from me, ' The Almighty wants payment of all the debt due by you.' And in an instant of time the angel Gabriel delivered the message, and the heart, before swollen so large, became small, and the vest slipped down, buttoned as it was.

From that day Huzrut Beebee Fatima became the most devoted of wives, and put away from her all pride, and performed her duties diligently without affectation or neglect, and was beloved of God and her husband.

Such is the story of the Lady Fatima, as the queen told it to us.

CHAPTER X.

PREJUDICES AND SUPERSTITIONS.

WISE and good as the queen was, death was
a subject which she would not allow to be
mentioned, or even alluded to, in her
presence. The word *death* was banished
altogether from ordinary conversation in her
household, and even its equivalents, to be
taken away, to depart this life, and such like,
were not used. The periphrasis by which
the idea was usually conveyed, was that the
responsibility of the child was off the parents'
shoulders, meaning that the child was dead ;
or the responsibility of the wife off the
husband's shoulders, meaning that the wife
was dead, and so on.

The queen's father or mother, I do not
know which, had died whilst apparently in a
sound sleep, and this had made such an
impression upon her mind when a girl, that

she always begged her attendants never to let her go into a very sound sleep, but to wake her up if she seemed to sleep more than ordinarily soundly. This the attendants always promised to do, but never did.

Her youngest son was about ten years of age when her husband, Umjid Aly Shah, died, and was a great favourite both with his father and mother. I remember, on one occasion, a large quantity of gold mohurs had been brought in by the queen's treasurer, and, having been counted, were arranged in little piles of ten each on the carpet in front of her. I was but a child, and the thought was in my mind that I had never seen such piles of gold before in all my life. The youngest son of the queen and his nurse came in just then, and as he was about my own age, or a little younger, I looked upon him with great interest. By and by there was a great disturbance. Some of the gold pieces were missing, and servants were suspected, and search was made, and all were in terror of flogging to extort confession. For two or three days the investigation and search about the missing gold went on, and both were unsuccessful—nothing was found.

At length the young prince himself told his mother he had taken some of the gold to give to his foster-mother, and that he had concealed it about his person before leaving the room. As many of the servants had been suspected, and so much trouble had been taken to find the culprit, the queen was very angry that her son had not told her before. So she had him tied hand and foot, after the manner of criminals, and taken into the king's presence to be judged and punished.

The king was at durbar when his son was brought to him thus; and on seeing the young prince, his favourite son, tied up, he was very angry, and ordered him to be released forthwith. He was very near punishing the servants who brought him in thus ignominiously, although they pleaded the queen's orders. However, finally, he released them with threats, and took the young prince and fondled him, and made him presents of gold and jewels.

The queen was not pleased at all this, and rated the king soundly when he next came to her apartment, and would not see the young prince for three days, as a punishment; but further punishment than that she did not or dared not inflict.

The queen was a believer in dreams, and no wonder. Do not thousands of dreams come true? A few months after the death of Umjid Aly Shah, the young prince, who had been very fond of his father, woke up one night crying, and said his father had called him three times. And the queen asked him, and the boy said, 'My father came to me and called to me three times thus, and beckoned: I want to go to him.' The young prince slept again; but the queen was very uneasy, and lay awake till morning. That morning the young prince got up, apparently quite well, but towards midday he sickened—cholera came on—and he was dead before evening! Yet people often say there is nothing in dreams!

It was not more than a year or so before the annexation of Oudh to the British territories in India, that the queen dreamt one night that an old man of venerable aspect had come to the king's durbar, and, taking the king her son by the hand, had lifted him off the royal carpet, leaving him to stand upon the floor beyond. As none in the household could interpret this dream, the soothsayers of Lucknow were collected, and, after much consultation, they decided that some serious injury threatened the kingdom, and they showed how it was to be averted by prayers, and gifts, and such like. But the means they showed to avert the danger failed ; and was not the annexation of Oudh by the English the fulfilment of the queen's dream ? Yet the impious laugh at dreams!

It was a tradition in the palace that women had been walled up, in more places than one, for infidelity, and other crimes, by the various kings ; and the queen had certain knowledge of two or three such cases that had occurred in former reigns. The queen therefore, did not like walking about the corridors or passages, after dark, and always had a good light in her own room. I have heard the queen say that more than once shrieks from the built-up walls had reached her ears, whether of the women themselves or of their spirits she did not know; and, so far as she could make out, they called for food, for water, for life. I was but a child, and often I had to go alone at night through these passages; and I went fearfully, my flesh creeping, my heart beating aloud, and every limb trembling—so much so that I could hardly walk.

After her widowhood the queen never occupied a state bed again, but simple couches of wood with little ornament. She always lay too on her right side, and her attendants said it was a penance she imposed on herself, in memory of her deceased husband.

So short had been the reigns of the two or three former kings of Oudh, that there was a rumour in Lucknow that a snake lay hidden in the throne, and that its poison soon ended the sovereign's life. Hence, when the queen's son Wajid Aly was crowned, he would not sit upon the *guddee*, or cushion, as his fathers had done, but simply touched the guddee seven times bowing, and then sat himself apart from it. And certain it is, that whilst his father and grandfather reigned only three or four years each, he reigned nine or ten years, and had many sons whilst·king. The throne in Lucknow was said to be the very one on which King Solomon, the wisest of men, had sat. It was taken to pieces by the English. Although the wisest of men had sat on that throne, all were not wise that sat on it. Wajid Aly had many wives, and so had Solomon. It is written in the Koran that Solomon had many wives, and he was the wisest of men, and it was God himself gave him his wisdom. Mashallah! God's will be done!

CHAPTER XI.

BORN IN THE PURPLE.

On the occasion of a birth in the royal harem, notice was sent to all the relatives of the father in the first place. None but female assistance and attendance were allowed, and the skill of these female attendants was proverbial. Drinks of hot milk, and food consisting of rice and pease flavoured with ginger and cloves, were the nourishment usually given in the first instance to the mother. If the infant was a son, cannon were fired, and fireworks let off at night with lavish profusion. If a daughter, the rejoicings were of a much milder and less boisterous character. For boys a wet-nurse was engaged for two years and a quarter, and for girls for one year and three-quarters, the mothers of the royal household never nursing their own children. Besides the wet-nurse, another woman was engaged whose sole duty it was to look after the wet-nurse, to see that she did not eat things likely to be injurious to her, and that she lived a strictly chaste and temperate life. This attendant was expected to be with the nurse night and day.

On the ninth day after the birth the mother was bathed and dressed in new clothes. Her friends were then first permitted to call upon her and offer their congratulations, and it was usual for her own relatives to forward gifts of large quantities of all kinds of food to the palace; the gifts of money and ornaments intended for the nurse were usually thrown into the bath-tub, on the occasion of the newly-born infant being first bathed—the father setting the example. After that first bath the infant was daily rubbed with oil, but was not again bathed for a whole year. The mother was similarly rubbed and shampooed with oil. Whether she were wife by *nikha* or *muta*—that is, by the most formal, or only by left-handed marriage—on the birth of a son she took rank at once after the duly betrothed and dowried wife. Her establishment was placed at once upon a more respectable footing, and she herself became a power in the state. But the giving birth to a daughter did not confer these advantages.

The mother on these occasions did not leave her room for forty days, and the mother of a son had then the liberty of roaming about in the palace, pretty much as she pleased, although her doing so previously would be highly indecorous—in fact, would not be permitted. The presents usually sent to the mother and child by the king were a cradle and playthings of silver, and ornaments for the wrists and ankles. The establishment with which a mother of a son was endowed comprised an annual payment from the treasury, larger or smaller in proportion to the favour in which she was held, but never to my knowledge less than 12,000 rupees a year (1,200*l*.). Handsome jewels and clothes were sent to her. She was addressed as *mulika*, or queen. Guards, attendants, slaves, were appointed for her, and she became at once the mistress of a household.

The name of the infant was usually chosen from the Koran, which was opened by the father or the moollah, as chance or fate decided, and the first word, or the first proper name, decided the matter. The moollah was often bribed to give a particular name, and then he made it appear that fate had decided it. Ill luck that, both for parent and child. Such a boy but too often sits heavily on the head of his father. Of course, there are good and bad moollahs, as there are good and bad men of all classes; but they ought to be the best of all men.

If the divination by opening the Koran fortuitously makes it appear that the son will be an injury to the father, the father is then forbidden to look upon it for one, two, or three months, as the case may be, to obviate the evil omen. The first bath of the mother is regulated as to the hour, and sometimes as to the day, by the divination from the Koran.

The apartment in which the birth has

taken place is held to be unclean for forty days. On the fortieth day it is thoroughly cleaned out, a chapter of the Koran read, and the woman is then permitted to join, for the first time since her confinement, in religious exercises.

The second son of the queen my mistress, usually called the general, who accompanied her to England and died there, was very dutiful to the queen, and both of them were fond of each other. One of his wives was the daughter of the vizier or prime minister, and to this wife he was not at all attached. In fact she seemed to be an object of aversion to him. The queen's only daughter was also married to the vizier's eldest son, and he retaliated the general's neglect of his sister upon his own wife, who was the general's sister. All this was the source of great trouble in the palace, and of much anxiety to the queen my mistress. Constant mediations were necessary on both sides, and it was not without the most earnest appeals on the queen's part that either of these husbands could be got to visit or live with these despised wives.

On one occasion, some five or six years before annexation, the general, in travelling, accidentally saw the two daughters of a poor Rajpoot (a Hindu). They were twelve and fourteen years of age respectively, and the general fell in love with them both. The queen saw them, and although they were Hindus, yet for the love she bore her son she consented to his marrying one of them. He took them both and married them. In course of time the eldest gave birth to a very beautiful boy, now with the ex-king at Calcutta, one of the handsomest children ever born in the palace. From the time that these two sisters had become the wives of the general, they had been dressed and educated as Mohammedans—the dress consisting of wide *pyjamas*, or drawers, each leg three four yards wide, an inner close-fitting vest, and a muslin sheet or veil, thrown over the head, and voluminous enough to envelope the entire figure if necessary. In adopting this dress, and in listening to and repeating the prayers from the Koran, the two sisters were regarded as having thrown away their pagan faith, Hinduism, and embraced the faith of the true believers.

In the midst of the joy at the birth of this son in the general's palace, the young mother began to long for a visit from her own mother, a poor Rajpoot woman. The general sent rich presents to the poor woman, and, having had her clothed in fine raiment, permitted her to come and visit her daughter. But the daughter was not content with this. The spirit of obstinacy was in her, and she insisted on her mother stopping with her altogether. This the general, as a good Mussulman, could not and would not permit. The young mother had set her heart upon this and upon nothing else. No rich presents nor jewels and ornaments, no, nor her own lovely son, could console her. She longed and pined and fretted herself to death. She died on the ninth day, and the general was inconsolable.

The queen loved her son the general, and was grieved at his distress. She sent through Lucknow and the provinces to try and get another beauty, Mussulman or Hindoo, equal to her he had lost. Many were brought, and the queen did her best to set off their attractions, and divert her son's mind from its sorrow, but all in vain. He would not be comforted.

Wearied at length with his obstinate grief, she spoke thus to him, one day that I was preparing the hookah for her, and he had come on a visit : ' What am I to do for you, unreasonable man ? Will nothing console you ? ' And he answered, ' If you could call her back from the tomb; that would console me ; but you cannot.' ' Then why did you let her pine and die ? ' asked the queen. ' When she was alive, was she not all your own ? Why not have allowed her mother to live with her ? ' ' Did I not let her mother visit her ? ' he asked, ' Could I do more ? Am I not a Mussulman ? '

Thus they spoke, after that, many times. However, he consoled himself, a year or so after, with another wife, and was happy.

I saw the son of that Rajpoot girl in Lucknow, a prisoner in the hands of the English after the mutiny. The English officer was

kind, and did not want to hurt the boy, and
sent him to the daughter of the vizier, the
general's wife, that wife whom he had
neglected so much. She would not receive
the youth, but returned him to the English
officer, reviling the boy as half a Hindu and
half a Christian, and saying that she had
nothing to do with him, and could not let
a child like that—and she called him an
opprobrious name—live with her. After
some delay and much correspondence, the
boy was finally sent down to Calcutta, and is
now with the ex-king, as I have said.

On the occasion of a birth in the palace,
particular care was taken to prevent evil
spirits doing any harm. For six days after
the infant's birth a fire and a light were kept
in the room constantly. The evil spirits are
driven away by fires and by lights—are they
not spirits of darkness, and of the Evil One?
But if human eyes are kept fixed on the little
one, the evil spirits have no power over it.
Hence a mother should never turn her back
upon her child for six days at least.

After I left the palace, during the time of

the wars, I was visiting a poor friend. A boy had just been born to her, and she had no proper assistance, and was wearied watching her little one, for fear of the spirits. So I took it from her, and told her to sleep, and she did so. I had travelled a good deal that day, and my eyes were heavy. However, determined to watch the little one, I sat on a low stool before a small fire, with my back to the wall, and the infant in my lap. After midnight, in spite of myself, I dozed, and, after a time, I heard a rushing footstep beating hard on the earthen floor, and I roused myself, and found the infant had been taken from my lap by the evil spirit, and was lying on the floor quite dead. The spirits take the life only, not the body. The child's neck was broken in the struggle. And you ask how I know it was an evil spirit did it. How do I know that I am alive now, and was alive then? Would God or a good spirit do it? No; the child could not have fallen from my lap, and broken its neck upon the hard unmatted ground. Besides, did I not hear the rushing footstep beating hard

upon the earthen floor? O full of unbelief!
—forgive me, my lord, but we in Oudh know
more of these evil spirits, and what they can
do, than you sahibs from England appear to
know. Did I not hear the footstep? Why
then talk of falling from my arms? Wah!
wah! but the world is as full of unbelief as
the sun is of light. But God is good and
great, and the evil spirits are very wicked.

CHAPTER XII.

HOLY MATRIMONY.

THE marriages in the court were of two kinds—*nikha* and *muta*. The former was the complete and perfect ceremony between equals; the latter usually between a superior and inferior, and not considered so binding as the nikha. In the royal family the boys were usually betrothed at the age of from ten to sixteen years. It was unusual to find a boy betrothed under ten years of age, and it would not have been easy to find a boy of sixteen who was not betrothed. The girls were usually betrothed when two years younger than the boys.

Presents of flowers and fruit usually passed between the betrothed until the time of marriage; and for a month before marriage the bride was fed exclusively upon milk, unleavened bread, and sweetmeats. Two days before the marriage both bride and bridegroom rubbed mayndee, a red dye, on the palms of their hands and the soles of their feet, and the way in which the mayndee adhered was considered emblematical of the lasting character of the affection between the two, and the happiness of the match. It was also usual for the bridegroom to send a suit of yellow clothing to the bride, as emblematical of love.

In the royal household all matters appertaining to dowry and such like were settled long before the marriage ceremony took place. But in the households of poorer Mussulmans it is not at all unusual for violent altercations on this subject to break out even when the marriage procession is being formed.

The marriage procession was usually a time of great mirth and festivity at court. Elephants with silver howdahs, splendid palanquins, and highly ornamented chairs of state borne by servants in liveries of scarlet and gold lace, bands of music, richly caparisoned horses, bearers of silver sticks (called *chob-dars*) and other bearers richly dressed, with trays of presents and sweetmeats of all kinds—all these, and crowds of thousands of citizens, formed a scene, when brilliantly lit up by torchlight, like that of the court of Indra and the Palace of the Peris.

This marriage procession, called the *bar-rath*, goes at night to conduct the bride to the house of the bridegroom. It usually started from the palace about eight or nine o'clock, and concluded about midnight. However near the houses might be to each other, the time consumed was the same, the procession going by a circuit when the houses were near, to lengthen out the ceremony. So with cannons firing, and fireworks blazing away, and torches flashing, so that night was turned into day, it stood before the door, awaiting the bride, whom the bridegroom had not yet seen. Nor did he see her till the ceremony was concluded.

The marriage ceremony—the nikha—is almost entirely religious. The parents answer for the girl, and the bridegroom engages to take her, to love her, to cherish her for ever, whether she be lovely and young, or old and blind and decrepit; whether black and·ugly, or fair and handsome. The bridegroom gives the nose-ring to the bride as the sign of marriage, but in the court a ring for the finger and a garland for the head were usually added.

At the close of the religious ceremony a muslin veil was thrown over the heads of both, and a mirror laid between them, in which the bridegroom, for the first time, saw the face of his bride. It was not difficult to judge, from the countenance of the youth when the veil was removed, whether he was pleased or disappointed. The bride was usually conducted to her own home again, that is, to the house of her father and mother, the following day, and lived with them a month or so, the bridegroom visiting her occasionally or regularly every day, remaining during the night and departing in the morning, according to his pleasure. From the devotion he exhibited during this first month, or from his indifference, the future well-being or unhappiness of the bride might be safely augured.

At the end of this month or so of probation the bride went finally to her husband's house to take her place in it as his wife. But it was not till after the birth of a son that she ruled as supreme in the household, and obtained full liberty of action. Till the birth of a son, for instance, she was not permitted to sit, converse, or eat with her husband, except in the privacy of her own apartment, if he chose to come there for that purpose. But the mother of a son, married by nikha, was female head of the household, and had in it almost absolute power. She could then visit her husband in his usual sitting-room, could join him at meals, and, in fact, act more like a wife according to the ideas of English sahibs.

One of the king's sons, who was afterwards killed in the streets of Lucknow during the mutiny, was little better than a fool, and offended his father so much by his wild silly behaviour, that he was usually under confinement. He was betrothed and married,

K

however, according to custom, and the girl
chosen for him was a nice quiet modest
well-looking bride, the daughter of one of
the inferior officers of the court. Everything
went on as usual until the muslin sheet was
thrown over them, and the mirror placed for
him to see her face. When this was done,
the band playing without in the courtyard,
all the assembled company was startled by a
piercing shriek from the bride, who fell down
insensible, having fainted from pain and
terror. The madman had torn her nose-
ring off, and bit her severely, whilst they
were concealed from view by the sheet. She
was rescued by her friends, was happily not
compelled to live with him, but lived and
died a virgin widow.

In the inferior left-handed muta marriages
so frequently contracted by the members of
the royal family, the bridegroom did not
appear in person. His sword and belt, or his
head-dress, or even some ornament of his
person, represented him on the occasion. The
usual form of words was gone through, but
no one regarded the ceremony as very bind-

ing or sacred. Binding it was on the part of the woman, who was liable to suffer death if false to her duty; but such marriages were easily dissolved by the king or his male relations, when they felt so disposed. On the birth of a son the muta wife usually, but not always, became nikha, and the nikha ceremony was gone through between her and her lord. This occurred several times in the reign of the ex-king Wajid Aly.

One of the muta wives of the king, who had been betrothed to a fellow villager, a playmate of hers, in infancy, escaped once in disguise from the palace. Direful was the commotion in consequence. Guards and attendants were flogged, and the shrieks resounded through the courtyards and corridors. Messengers were despatched in various directions to bring back the fugitive. She was found and brought back on the third day. I saw her after that for the first time. She had large black eyes, an oval face, and a fair complexion. Her features were regular, but wanted expression—all except the eyes, which seemed to look through one, so piercing and lustrous were they, swimming as if in a sea of passion.

Instead of punishing her terribly, as we all expected he would, the king seemed to pay her more attention than usual on her return; indeed so much so, that one day the queen my mistress remonstrated with him. 'She is but a villager,' said the queen: 'instead of indulgence, she deserves punishment; and you grant her all her desires.' 'I grant her none of her desires,' was the king's reply; 'she will not express a wish for anything. I cannot make her out. Her eyes are full of fire, and all the rest is as a marble statue. She interests me. I offer her jewels and ornaments; she says she does not want them. I get dancing girls for her amusement; she looks on and smiles not. A villager! Yes, she is a villager. But, by the beard of the Prophet, she knows how to act the queen!'

The queen my mistress said no more. When the king her son swore by the beard of the Prophet she was not pleased, for she was pious, and liked not profane oaths.

A month rolled on, and still this muta

wife, the villager, was made much of. She
was not liked. She had made no friends in
the court, for she spoke scarcely at all. At the
end of about a month after the conversation
I have related, she disappeared altogether—
but this time it was the king's vengeance
caused her disappearance, not her own flight.
I forget her name, and cannot tell what her
fate was, but I am sure it was dreadful. The
king had done his best to please and amuse
her, and she would not be pleased or amused.
I heard too that she openly told him she
loved the village youth to whom she had
been betrothed, and did not love him the
king! If so, what could she expect? Kings
will not be treated in that way by village
girls. The young man to whom she had
been betrothed suffered with her. I do not
know what his fault was. Perhaps he had
enticed her to leave the palace when she
escaped disguised. I do not know. I only
know that his mother came to the queen
to complain of the loss of her son, and for
nearly a month sat at the gate wailing, with
ashes on her head, and demanding justice

and mercy. She gave a great deal of trouble, poor thing! I could not help pitying her. Whether the queen asked the king her son anything about the young man, I do not know. She did not talk of the matter before me. Perhaps she knew all about the case beforehand. Whatever was the true explanation, all I know about it is this, that she ordered money to be given to the poor woman, and that she should be sent back to her village. Yes! she was a good and kind queen. If there was any fault in this affair, it was not hers, but the king's. Who can resist their fate?

CHAPTER XIII.

THE ANGEL OF DEATH.

As the body becomes unclean the moment
life departs, the relatives and friends hasten
to leave the apartment, when assured that
the angel of death has taken possession of it.
Those employed at court to wash the body
were Syuds, and took the corpse into a bath-
room for that purpose, women ministering to
women, and men to men. Some ornament—
a ring on the finger, or a wristlet on the arm
—was usually left, that the deceased might
not enter empty-handed into Paradise.

A coffin was used to carry the corpse to
the grave, but was not buried with it. The
body was rolled in a new piece of white
cloth, and laid in the coffin, and when the
funeral procession took place, a pall or
canopy of rich cloth, supported on the ends

of four poles, was carried by four mourners over the coffin. It is not well that heaven should look upon a bare coffin. Arrived at the grave, the body was taken from the coffin, and the moollah read the Koran, and a man went into the grave, and placed two sticks across (in the form of a St. Andrew's cross), leaning on the head of the grave, against which the deceased might rest, when sitting up to be examined by the angels Monker and Nikel, on the third day.

Held by the head and the feet, the body was then placed in the grave, and boards so arranged at some distance above it as to prevent the earth falling upon the corpse. The funeral party then retired forty paces for some minutes, and returned and looked in, to see that no change had taken place, before filling up the grave. Finally, a whisper for his eternal salvation was breathed into the ear of the corpse; the nearest of kin threw in the first clod of earth, and the grave was filled up.

Fires were then lit at the foot and at the head of the grave, to keep off evil spirits, for do not the spirits of darkness avoid the light? The Koran was daily read, and the relatives returned daily at day-dawn to pray. On the morning of the third day, the ceremony called *thujah* was performed; the friends took bread and cakes, flour and oil and cardamums, and, having kindled a fire, threw sweetmeats and flour and portions of bread into the flames, in the name of the deceased. Then, dipping their thumbs and little fingers into the oil, they touched their tongues and ears with it, still mentioning the name of the deceased. Lastly, the provisions were dropped bit by bit into the flames, the name being repeated as each morsel was thrown in. The thujah performed, the relatives went to the grave, and a moollah, or the nearest of kin, called out aloud to the deceased, 'How is it with you in the other world? Have you been well received?' The sounds first heard after asking these questions were taken as the answer. Sounds of mirth or joy or lightness of heart or singing of birds indicating happiness, and sounds of woe indicating misery.

A jar of water, and a cake or two of unleavened bread, were placed every morning
by the grave for forty days, and prayers
were read daily for the same length of time,
and the mourning continued as long, in ordinary cases; but there were many exceptions
to this rule. The queen my mistress had
lights, and the Koran read, at the grave of
her husband, Umjid Aly Shah, for many
months.

During this time of mourning, the hair is
not oiled, nor is the beard or the head
shaven, nor are the clothes washed, nor is
soormah (black dye) used to adorn the eyes,
nor is pawn eaten. And the widow mourns,
with covered face, in white clothing, and
wears no ornaments. Often has the queen
said, if widows did their duty they would not
marry again, but would mourn all their lives
for their lords. But surely the world is wicked
now, and the widow hastens to remarry,
and her friends help her in this naughtiness!

The death of the king was in this wise—
When the king, Umjid Aly Shah, felt his
end approaching, he ordered the council-

chamber to be prepared, and fresh carpets to be spread, and new cushions; and he had his beard trimmed, and put on new and splendid clothing, and, having lain down in the council-chamber, he sent for the queen. There they both wept, and he spoke much to her in whispers. The boil or ulcer on his shoulder at that time was as large as a saucer, and the flesh all eaten away, it was said, from some poisonous ointment given by the physician. How can I tell if the report was true? Such was the rumour in the palace, and of course the physician would not have dared to do so of himself. He must have been bribed to it.

When the king and the queen were weeping, then all the attendants wept; and I was but a girl, yet I remember how sad a sight it was. I was in attendance on the queen at this time, and was near the door, having followed her with other servants. And I was told the king said to the queen, 'Beware of putting Wajid Aly on the throne; if you do, all the family will perish, and your heart will be broken.' But what could the queen do?

The vizier and the English resident did as they pleased, and Wajid Aly was made king.

After much whispering talk, he said he would sleep, and the queen laid down his head gently, and covered it. The attendants, suspecting he was dead, got her away with great difficulty, and she thought he was still sleeping; but he was dead. He died, like a king, in his royal robes, on his throne, in his council-chamber.

And then the news went to the English resident, and the followers of Wajid Aly, the heir-apparent, hailed him as king, and the voice of wailing was drowned in the shouts of gladness; and the timbrel, the sytar, and the drum, were played and beaten; and the new king put on royal robes, and his mother, the queen, was summoned to go to the emanbarrah (the Moslem cathedral), with the vizier and the English resident, that he might be crowned at once. So the body of the dead king, Umjid Aly Shah, was left to servants alone. All was joy and commotion, and cannons firing, and bands playing without, whilst the servants were preparing for the burial of the dead within.

The queen was detained long at the eman-barrah, nor was she allowed to return till the coronation was over, and all the court lords had taken the oaths of allegiance. It was past midnight before all this was over and she got back, and the king, Umjid Aly Shah, had died early in the day, before noon. Why his funeral was hurried over I do not know. Probably the new king had given orders to that effect. But, shortly after it was dark, the corpse was carried out. Pall-bearers, and the grave, and all were ready. So, before the queen returned from the coronation, the funeral was over.

Many were the whispers of foul play in the palace, and some that are older than I am, and were fully grown at the time, say that there is no doubt there *was* foul play. But what do I know? I was but a child.

I remember that, some time after, the queen my mistress reproved her son for having his own image stamped on the coinage of his father, after having had his father's image defaced. The queen said, 'Have a new coinage, with your own image and superscription, made; but deface not the image of your father. How shall that son obtain the favour of heaven who mars his father's work?'

There is no doubt that women were put to death in the palace for infidelity to their lords, and why should they not? But I never saw any of them put to death. They were sometimes flogged, too, for minor offences, and the floggings in the palace were terribly severe. That several had been walled up in the palace, buried alive, there can be no doubt. The queen often spoke of them, and after the death of her husband she would not go about at night in consequence. But I believe the commonest death was beheading, or being shot by the female guards of the palace. I do not believe that any women were walled up or buried alive during my time in the palace. The queen my mistress would not have allowed it. Her influence in the state was very great, and the king her son always consulted her in political matters.

As to the way in which the women were

walled up, I have already said I never saw
it, but I have heard the queen talk of it.
The arms and the feet of the victim were
tied, and a string united the two. This
string was attached to a bolt or iron ring,
prepared for the purpose in the wall, and
another string was passed round the waist,
and attached to the same bolt or ring behind.
The victim thus stood up, with her back to
the wall, usually in a corner or recess, her
head being uncovered. Masons attached to
the palace, or eunuchs who had learned the
art of masonry, then commenced to build a
wall from the floor upwards—a stout, sub-
stantial wall, to shut up the victim in her
tomb alive; cutting off a corner, or merely
filling up a recess thereby, so that no injury
was done to the room. It must have been
terrible to the victim as the bricks rose
higher and higher—to her waist, her breast,
her eyes—till all light was shut out, and with
it all hope. God is great; and may God and
the Prophet preserve us from sin!

CHAPTER XIV.

AMUSEMENTS AT COURT.

THE QUEEN cared little for amusement after the death of her husband Umjid Aly Shah. She would sit for hours at night poring over the Koran. The story-tellers' tales were her chief pleasure.

But Wajid Aly her son, the ex-king, was very fond of games and amusements of all kinds, and of music and singing and dancing. Even during the lifetime of his father, Wajid Aly would often dress as a female, and amuse the ladies of the harem by dancing as a woman. But this was done secretly at that time, he knew his father would not approve of it. When he became king, however, of course he did exactly as he pleased. He wrote much poetry, chiefly love songs, in very choice Persian and Urdu, and filled up all his leisure hours with music and dancing, greatly to the disgust of the queen his mother.

In one of the months of the cold weather annually he had a play acted in his household, in which he and the ladies of the court took part, and which I saw several times. This play represented the abduction of a very beautiful girl, called Ghyzalah, by an evil monster (one of the genii of Arabic tales), and her subsequent restoration by Rajah Indra.

One of the king's wives was annually chosen to represent Ghyzalah, and, as she was very beautiful, the honour of representing her was eagerly sought in the harem; others were dressed as peris, with silver wings. Another represented Rajah Indra (the king of the peris, or fairies of Hindu mythology). Others were dressed up as evil genii and their attendants, with black ornaments and black wings and blackened faces. None wished to act these last parts, but at the expression of the king's wishes none could refuse.

The play was acted in the silver bara-

L

dhurry of the Kaiser Bagh palace in Lucknow, which was divided for the purpose into three compartments. One of these compartments was richly decorated and fitted up as Rajah Indra's court, the pillars being covered with silver paper, and the richest ornaments lavished on the ceiling and walls, whilst at night it was a blaze of light with chandeliers and mirrors. In the centre was Indra's throne, and there the lady representing him sat in state in the richest apparel, attended by crowds of peris. It was a beautiful sight. Whilst all this was going on within, fountains without were playing scented waters, and the richest and choicest flowers were in the garden near. The seats of the garden were gilded or silvered over, so as to shine amid the flowers and fountains; in the daytime the sun's rays lit up the whole, and in the night thousands of lamps. The play lasted ten days, and for ten days and nights this gorgeous scene continued.

In another compartment a room was fitted up as a royal bedroom, and, on the first day of the play, Ghyzalah, beautiful as a houri, was seen lying on a rich couch, as if asleep, beside the king, who represented her husband. They lay so half the day, and all the household crowded to see. Wah! wah! but it was a sight worth seeing—the golden bedstead, and the rich counterpane, and the magnificent carpet, and the golden furniture, and the beautiful Ghyzalah, her delicate limbs in gauze or muslin edged with golden tissue, and her black hair shining with gems —altogether most lovely. Beside her lay the king, fat and burly, but in gorgeous apparel.

At length the king leaves the couch, and the black attendants of the evil genius carry off both the couch and Ghyzalah, and hide the lady.

As soon as the king, who acts the husband of Ghyzalah, becomes aware of the loss, he sets out as a fakir or jogee to seek her. Almost naked, with his body painted, and only a cloth round his loins, a staff in his hand, and a wallet by his side, he goes all over the palace, avoiding only the court of Indra in the baradhurry, shouting out, ' Hay Ghyzalah! hay Ghyzalah!' His wife Khash

Mehal, in the dress of sadness, of a light brown colour, accompanied him, and all the household not engaged in the play wore garments of the same colour for two days.

The queen my mistress, at first refused to wear this dress of sadness herself, or to supply her household with it, but after a couple of years the king urged her so earnestly that she consented, protesting at the same time against the folly of the whole affair.

Through the gardens, and along the corridors, and from room to room, went the king, as a fakir, looking for Ghyzalah, and shouting 'Hay Ghyzalah! hay Ghyzalah!' attended by Khash Mehal in the dress of sadness, and by other women.

All Lucknow was obliged to dress in garments of the prescribed colour, a light brown, during this search, and I believe an edict was issued, that anyone appearing in clothes of another colour should be imprisoned.

In the mean time Ghyzalah had been taken to the court of Rajah Indra, in the baradhurry. She was received there with great warmth by Rajah Indra, who wanted her to become one of his peris, and a good deal of the fun of the piece consisted in the love shown by Rajah Indra to Ghyzalah— everyone being aware that this Rajah Indra was not a man at all, but only a woman dressed up. Boppery bop! but it was a glorious sight!

At length, when the fakir, wearied and dispirited with his fruitless search, has been supposed to have visited all the world, and to have searched every kingdom, for the lost Ghyzalah, one of the attendants of the evil genii, relenting on seeing the devotion of her husband, comes to him, and, having extorted many promises, informs him where the lost fair one is.

Bounding with joy, the fakir and his train visit the court of Indra, and they behold the beautiful Ghyzalah, on a seat beside the supposed god, and being fondled by him. Then begins a long colloquy, in which at length Indra promises to restore Ghyzalah, if her husband will prove his worth in various ways —as a warrior, as a hunter, as a lover, as a musician, and as a dancer.

Marvellous was the sight when the fakir issued forth next day as a warrior, in shining armour, to prove his military prowess. He vanquishes one after another of the black attendants of the evil genii, and all the court of Indra applauds, and attend him daintily to his couch, to divest him of his beautiful armour. As a hunter, as a lover, as a musician, as a dancer, he is equally successful; and, amidst the loud plaudits of the entire assembly, he receives back his bride, the beautiful Ghyzalah, and conducts her to the royal chamber from which she was first stolen away.

The same scene with which the play opens, concludes it.

It was the custom of the king, however, on the tenth day, to dance in the baradhurry for the entertainment of the multitude, and he insisted upon the queen, and Khash Mehal, and other leading ladies of court, giving him presents in money on the termination of the entertainment. On one occasion I remember the queen my mistress gave him a donation of 3,000 rupees (300l.), with which he was well pleased.

Another amusement of the court, in which the king took great interest, was a kind of play between him and the king of the peris (*amil-i-jinnut*). Who this king of the peris was, or where he came from, I never could make out, but he certainly did wonderful things, and people consulted him about sickness, and about troubles and misfortunes, and got wonderful answers and great relief. Wah! wah! but it was marvellous.

Several of the singers and natch-girls were dressed up as peris, and attended their king when the play took place. They would surround the throne of their king, who acted his part with great dignity; and, after we had all seen the king and his throne, the door would be shut, and the peris remained within with him whilst we were excluded. Then our king came from his own apartments, in his royal robes. He was a fine stout man, not more than thirty years of age, but he looked much older; and his attendants knocked at the door, and after some talk it was opened, and behold! the king of the peris and his throne were both gone, and were nowhere to be seen, whilst all the rest remained as it was in the room! No, there was no door by which he could have got out. There was only one door, and near that we were all gathered. He could not have got out that way without our seeing him. And the windows were very small and high up—too small for a man to get out. Nor was there any hole in the floor, all was solid masonry. No, there are many things too wonderful to be explained, and this is one of them. There are spirits good and bad, and some men can get their help to do wonderful things.

Then our king entered, and a rich carpet and cushion were brought for him, and a pillow against which to lean, just as in the durbar; and he sat there, and a voice from the air gave him the salutation, 'Salaam aleikum!' (peace be with you), and the king answered. It was the king of the peris gave the salutation, but he was invisible, and his voice appeared to come from overhead. God is great, and with the help of spirits wonderful things can be done. No, it was not any of the peris standing about that gave the salutation. It was the voice of a man, that man whom we had seen sitting on the throne, and now man and throne were both invisible.

And after much dancing and singing of the peris before the king, *our* king, there was again a colloquy between our king and the invisible; and the king of the peris promised to come down to his brother, our king, and to sit and converse with him.

So the door was again shut. Bismillah! but it was a wonderful thing and an inexplicable. When we were admitted again, the king of the peris was there upon his throne, just as he had been before, talking to our king Wajid Aly. Where could he have come from but from the air, in which he had been invisible? Do I tell lies? Did I alone see it? Did not hundreds witness it as well as I? If I saw it not with these eyes, may my life and death be both unfortunate.

A general dance, with music and singing, in which our king took part, and the king of the peris. loudly applauded him, concluded the entertainment.

CHAPTER XV.

THE QUEEN'S FAVOURITE STORY.

BEFORE beginning a story, the story-teller always repeated the following lines :—

> Sleeps all the world—
> Waking is God alone—
> This tale is not so false,
> Nor are its words so sweet—
> Eyes of mine saw it not,
> From hearsay I repeat it.
> Of him who hath composed it,
> False or true, the meed be his.

And of all the stories the queen heard, the following was the one she most liked, and which she had most frequently repeated to her :—

There was a king who was becoming old without having had any son. Indeed he had no children ; his wife was barren. One day he called his vizier to him, and asked his

advice. Now the vizier was a wise man and
skilful, and he said, 'In the middle of a
great jungle far, far off, many hundreds of
miles away, lives a holy Fakir. He sits at
the foot of a great mango-tree, and sleeps
twelve years at a time, waking also for the
same length of time; and he is surrounded
by spirits and ogres of superhuman power,
who carefully protect him from the intrusion
of mankind. This Fakir knows all enchant-
ments, and one of the mangoes from his holy
tree will cure any disease, and remove bar-
renness.'

So next day the king sat in durbar in
great state, and summoned all his nobles and
the officers of his army and of his household, and told them what the vizier had said.
But all were afraid, and not one offered to
face the perils of the way, and procure for
the king one of the enchanted mangoes, or
the Fakir's advice.

Then the king asked if there was any
man ready to risk his life in this service;
and they all, with one voice, every man of
them, said, 'I am ready.'

So the king had a glass of sherbet and a plate of salt brought into the divan, and said, 'Whoever undertakes this work must devote himself to it by drinking the sherbet and tasting the salt.' Every man sat still. No man stirred. All were afraid.

At length the vizier himself, stepping forward, pledged himself to the enterprise, and drank the sherbet and tasted the salt. When he had so done every man in the divan lifted up his voice and said, 'I too am ready.' But the king, despising vain words, arose from his throne and embraced the vizier as a brother, and kissed him, and promised him half the kingdom on his return.

So the vizier set his house in order, and went forth, with camp and followers, on his long journey, the king escorting him, with great pomp and splendour, to the gates of the town.

Many weary days did the vizier journey on, now crossing plains, now mountains, another time deep and rapid rivers, and again pathless jungles; but his heart was good, and God was with him.

Wearied with a long day's march, he threw himself down one evening under a tree to rest himself, and as he was trying to go to sleep he heard a parrot and a mina (a kind of magpie) conversing in the tree above his head; and he knew the language of birds, and listened, and lo! they were talking of him.

'Great is the sorrow of the king,' said the mina, 'and great the valour of the vizier; but alas! it is all of no avail. He will never reach the Fakir.'

'Why so, my brother?' asked the parrot.

'Because there is a deep broad rapid river before him, on which no boat ever swam, and beyond that for a hundred miles the country is defended by ogres and evil spirits, whom no man can pass, and they watch day and night.'

'The vizier doubtless relies on God,' said the parrot.

So the vizier was comforted by what the parrot said, and turned and slept soundly, and with a bold heart set forward next day on his journey again, for his motives and conscience were good.

And after journeying many days the vizier came at length to the mighty river which no man could pass, so broad and deep and rapid was it, and on it no boat had ever floated. There was no bridge, no human being appeared, nothing but the mass of water rolling dark eternally on; and for a time the vizier's heart sank within him, and he wept. But anon he remembered what the parrot had said, 'The vizier doubtless relies on God,' and he dismissed his fears, and felt stout of heart again, and prayed to Heaven to help him. Now his motives and his conscience were good, and Heaven heard his prayer, and he heard a voice saying to him, 'Be not afraid, walk straight on.'

Right in front of him was the world of waters, and for a moment his heart shrivelled up within him, as a leaf is shrivelled up by the fire; but it was only for a moment, and saying to himself, 'I trust in God,' he walked into the waters.

Behold, the angel Gabriel was with him, and bore him across the river safe to the other side.

And when they had arrived at the other side, the angel Gabriel said to him, 'Thou didst trust in God, and thy faith is rewarded. What seekest thou?'

So he told the whole story, and why he had come, to the angel, and the angel said, 'Dost thou know that for a hundred miles round the Fakir ogres and evil spirits guard the territory, and no human foot can pass them? They sleep not day or night.'

'I trust in God,' was the vizier's reply.

So the angel was much pleased, and gave the vizier two packets—a packet of fire and a packet of water — with instructions how to use them, and left him to go on his way rejoicing.

And now the vizier entered a thick dark forest, wherein was no path, but the angel had told him how to proceed, and by the sun in the daytime and by the stars at night he guided himself ever onwards, straight towards the Fakir, never sleeping or slumbering for this hundred miles.

And as he went on one dark night, no

light but that of the stars visible, and they but dim, he heard mutterings as of evil spirits in front of him, and on his right hand, and on his left, and behind him. In his hand he had his staff, and, though his flesh crept and his hair stood on end, he went ever onwards through the dark forest. And the mutterings increased to thunder, and lightnings played about him, and trees fell, and last of all, frightful awful shapes began to appear—such shapes as would terrify mankind in crowds by day, and the vizier was alone in a thick forest by night.

Last of all, a mouth of fire, like the opening of a great furnace, glared before him, with large yellow saucer eyes above it, all alight with hate and fury, and the mouth drew near as if to swallow him, whilst he saw a thousand claws, as of lions, tigers, and bears, ready to drag his body asunder.

Shouting out, 'I trust in God!' the vizier scattered the packet of fire around him, as the angel had directed, and the ogres and evil spirits were burnt up, and the vizier was saved from that danger.

But, saved though he was from the ogres and the evil spirits, another danger awaited him. The fire, which had consumed them, seized upon the trees and the brushwood around, and a great conflagration blazed on every side, and the vizier was nearly suffocated with the smoke, and saw the fire ever drawing nearer. Then he bethought him of the packet of water, and he scattered it around; and the water spread over the fire, and extinguished it, and then swept on in a body towards the great river.

Wearied and faint with his excessive labours, the vizier repeated, 'I trust in God!' and found himself on the further verge of the great forest at daybreak, and a plain before him, in the centre of which rose the mango-tree, under which the Fakir was sitting. And the air of this plain removed all his weariness at once, and he felt fresh and strong and active, and gave praise and glory to God.

Now the Fakir was a very old man, and his appearance was dreadful, so that no man without faith could look on him and retain his senses. Grass and shrubs grew all over

M

the Fakir, and his long white hair fell to the ground, and, as he sat, his eyelashes, when cast down, touched the ground, and all about him was strange and weird and awful.

Birds of beautiful plumage and exquisite song were in large numbers in the mango-tree above him.

The vizier came before the Fakir salaaming low, and as the Fakir took no notice, the vizier stood on one foot, with hands joined, in the attitude of submission and request, in front of the Fakir.

The vizier still trusted in God, and the Fakir still took no notice of him.

Then, for four-and-twenty hours the vizier so stood, without food and without drink. When the four-and-twenty hours had elapsed, the Fakir raised his long eyelashes, and with open eyes looked at the vizier for an hour, and then said :—

'What do you want?'

The voice was as thunder, or as the rolling of distant drums—a voice to strike awe and terror into man's heart. But the vizier trusted in God, and answered bravely, and told the fakir all that was in his heart, and wherefore he had come.

Then the Fakir took his great staff up, and gave it to the 'vizier, and said :—

'Strike the mango-tree one blow, and whatsoever falls from it is yours. Take it, and begone, and trouble me no more.'

So the vizier did as he had been directed, and took the staff, and struck the tree one blow. Two mangoes fell, and the vizier quickly took them up, and fastened them in his waistband, and laid the staff by the Fakir's side, and made his obeisance. But the Fakir heeded him not, his eyes were again on the ground, and his long eyelashes drooping down covered them.

So the vizier praised God, and turned on his way back rejoicing.

The magical virtue of the mangoes made the way light and easy to him. He encountered no dangers. The angel Gabriel again assisted him at the river. At the other side he found his horse and attendants, and went on his way back rejoicing.

The fame of his return spread to the court

of the king, who came out a day's journey to meet him, bringing with him all the courtiers who had been at the durbar, and who had been afraid to undertake the expedition. And when the king spoke to them of it, they all answered with one voice, 'We too were all ready to go.'

The vizier gave the king one of the mangoes, and kept the other for his own wife, who was also barren.

So the queen ate the mango, and in due time a son was born to her—a fine hearty healthy boy—and the king was wild with delight. The vizier got half the kingdom, and the country was all a scene of rejoicing, and the king opened his treasury for three days, so that all the poor might help themselves.

When the soothsayers and the astrologers were collected together to prepare the boy's horoscope, then the king was sad again, for the wise men told him that the boy would be heavy on his father's head for nine years and nine months and nine days. When that period was once passed, then all danger was over. So the king sorrowfully had a beautiful palace built for the prince, with high walls all round, and in this was all that could delight the boy, or minister to his happiness; and daily, almost hourly, the king got news of his son's welfare.

Now the vizier's wife had had a daughter, beautiful as a peri, and she was similarly brought up in the other half of the kingdom. Both were instructed in all learning, and were good as they were learned and clever.

When the fated period had passed away, the young prince was received in court with great rejoicings, and lived happily for some years with his father.

One day, in passing through the bazaar, he saw Biswa Lukhy, a beautiful young female, seated on the roof of a house. Their eyes met, and they were in love. She was not a girl of a reputable life; but she fascinated the prince, and he spent with her all the hours he could spare from the palace, keeping the matter a secret from his father and mother.

So things were in this state when the

parents of the prince thought of marrying him, and they chose the daughter of the vizier, who had half the kingdom, and this daughter was beautiful as a peri. By this marriage all would be made happy, and the kingdom would be reunited into one.

So the portrait of the prince was sent to the court of the vizier, and the portrait of the vizier's daughter, all set in diamonds, was sent back. The diamonds were rich and beautiful, but the eyes and features of the face represented in this portrait were brighter and more beautiful than the diamonds. The king and queen were charmed with the portrait, and sent for their son to come and see it. But he was in the bazaar with Biswa Lukhy, by whom he had been fascinated.

Now Biswa Lukhy knew all that was going on, and had heard of the arrival of the beautiful portrait, and detained the prince on purpose, plotting with her friends how to destroy the portrait before the prince should see it.

So Biswa Lukhy sent for seven old witches renowned in that town, and, after hearing their own accounts of what they could each

do, chose one of them, told her what she
wanted, and promised her rich rewards if
she would so deface the portrait, or mar its
beauty, that the prince would have no long-
ing to see the original.

The witch went off to perform what was
desired, and, having torn her clothes and
put ashes on her head, she sat down, weeping and wailing, under the balcony where the
queen used to sit.

The queen sent an attendant to enquire
the cause of her sorrow, and the witch
replied that if the queen would let her
come into the presence she would detail
it all, not otherwise. The queen admitted
her, and she proceeded to tell a sad tale of
family loss and bereavement, as having
happened in the city where the vizier held
his court, and the young princess lived.

The queen then gave the witch money,
and said, ' You have seen the princess, then ? '

' Every day for years,' was the reply, ' Did I
not daily go to the vizier's palace till I lost
my son ? '

So the queen got out the portrait, and

proceeded to take off its numerous wrappings to show it to the witch, and asked if it was like the princess.

The witch, pretending she could not see it properly in the room, took the portrait outside into the verandah, and there with colour prepared for the purpose she quickly destroyed the lustre of the eyes, and rendered the mouth ugly. Then, hastily wrapping it up again, as she was bringing it in, she said to the queen that it was exactly like the princess, who was beautiful as one of the peris of the court of Indra.

Then, after some further conversation, the old witch, child of the devil, made many obeisances, and took her leave.

The prince soon after came in, and the queen his mother put the portrait into his hands at once, telling him to keep it till he should obtain possession of the princess as his bride. He took the portrait to his own apartments, and, opening it, saw a picture of a girl, blear-eyed and ugly mouthed, in rich apparel, and he did not long to see the original. But being a dutiful son, and knowing that it was of advantage to have the kingdom reunited again, he made no opposition to the marriage, resolving in his own mind, however, that Biswa Lukhy should have still all his devotion.

As the day drew near for the bridegroom's procession to go and meet the bride, and bring her home, Biswa Lukhy pretended to be taken ill with fear and anxiety, and would not be comforted till the prince promised to wear a bandage over his eyes, under the wedding garland that always adorned the bridegroom's head, and not to look upon his bride till she, Biswa Lukhy, gave him leave.

It was a very sad wedding for the young bride, who began to fear that her husband was blind, and that the fact had been purposely concealed. However, like her father the vizier, she trusted in God.

Some months passed away, and the young prince spent his time with Biswa Lukhy; and his young bride and his father and his mother were all equally sorry: but still he had never seen his bride, for Biswa Lukhy had not permitted him, and he kept his promise. And his bride was ever more beautiful and more sad.

At length the princess made up a scheme of her own, and got her father-in-law, the king, to help her in carrying it out. He got an old palace of his in the city, not far from where Biswa Lukhy lived, fitted up, and the princess went to live there. And the king ordered all the milkwomen to remove to the neighbourhood of that palace, and thither they removed and lived there, so that it was called the milkwomen's quarter.

So the princess got a rich dress of many-coloured silk woven for herself, and made up in the manner of the dresses worn by the Hindu milkwomen—full round the waist, and the end crossing over the breast, from the right side to the left shoulder, and then over the head, hanging down to the waist. And she had ornaments, the same as the Hindu milk-sellers wore, made, but of the richest materials, and a pitcher of gold, light and beautiful, but still like the brass vessels in which the Hindu milkwomen carried the milk about.

Having got all these things prepared, she took her pitcher of milk, and drew her veil over her face, and she went towards the house where Biswa Lukhy lived, and there, just under the window, she began to sing—

Come, buy my milk,
  Or good or bad ;
Come buy my milk,
  And make me glad.
Nor rest, nor peace,
  Nor joy is won,
Nor sorrows cease,
  Till work is done.
Then buy my milk,
  Or good or bad ;
Come buy my milk,
  And make me glad.

The prince heard this strange song, so different from the usual puffing up of the seller's wares—heard it and wondered, and went, simply from curiosity, to the window, to see the milkwoman. Her appearance surprised him—the rich dress, and the beauty of the form—so he sent for her, and asked the price of her vessel of milk. He could not see her face, which was veiled, but he was pleased with the grace of her demeanour and the modesty of her manner. 'The price of my milk is the full of this vessel of silver,' was the answer to his question.

He had the milk taken and the vessel filled with silver in return, and then addressed her in poetry gaily—

Come with joy and gladness,
　All gloom away we'll chase;
Here put aside your sadness,
　And unveil your pretty face.

But her answer was—

My milk is sold,
　My work is done;
My face I hold
　My lord's alone.

So saying she departed, and Biswa Lukhy was sulky that day, seeing the impression that the milkmaid had made.

The next day the princess came again, and the same scene was repeated, and Biswa Lukhy was still more angry.

The third day the princess came again, and the same scene was repeated, and Biswa Lukhy could not restrain her rage, but would have struck the pretended milkmaid, only that the prince prevented it, and, to take the more care òf her, followed her to the milk-women's quarter. There, as she was entering a side door of one of the outhouses of the palace in which she lived, the prince again addressed her softly in poetry once more—

> Thy form is fair,
> Thy jewels rare;
> But what thy face,
> I cannot trace.
> With envious fold
> Thy veil doth hold
> Its beauty hid,
> My glance forbid.
> Then be thou kind,
> And ease my mind;
> Thy home, thy name,
> Thy state proclaim.

And the maiden-wife answered him kindly, and said—

> Not now I reveal to thee,
> Or make it all clear;
> Return in the night to me,
> And all thou shalt hear.

So saying she went rapidly inside, and the prince, taking note of the door, returned as soon as the light of day had departed, and night had set in.

In the mean time the princess had prepared everything for his reception. The sitting-rooms were decorated with the richest carpets, and mirrors were on the walls, and chandeliers hung from the roof, multiplied a thousandfold by the mirrors on all sides, and a magnificent banquet was spread out in the dining room. In her own room, all that art and luxury could do to render the scene enchanting was accomplished, whilst delicious perfumes were wafted abroad from golden censers, and soft music played at a distance. The princess herself was in her costliest apparel, every beauty heightened by art, and the rich raven tresses of her hair adorned with flowers and gems, whilst her cheeks became red and pale by turns as she thought of her husband and her love.

At length, as she was impatiently waiting in her own apartment, a eunuch, who had been stationed there for the purpose, introduced him into the sitting-room, and he was amazed at the wealth and luxury of the scene. But when the princess herself, in all the blaze of her beauty, appeared before him, he forgot everything else, and would have fondled her in his arms, thinking it was only the milk-maid still. She repelled him, however, and would suffer no embrace until all was known and all revealed. They sat opposite to each other; a female story-teller was introduced and began to give a history of a prince and princess, a history similar to theirs, and as the story proceeded the prince knew who she was, and, telling the story-teller to depart, pressed the princess to his heart, and heaven smiled upon their virtuous love.

Next morning he sent for Biswa Lukhy, and, embracing his wife, reproached the evil doer for having kept him so long from so much happiness; and then, turning to his wife, he said : ' Now choose the manner of her death, my love. Shall she be buried alive, or shot to death with poisoned arrows, or torn into four pieces with wild horses ? ' But the princess would not choose, leaving it to her lord to do as seemed good to him. So the prince had Biswa Lukhy first buried alive, care having been taken to give her air enough to live for twenty-four hours, and when the twenty-four hours were completed, and she had felt the bitterness of that death, then she was taken out, and shot at with poisoned arrows, the prince himself putting an arrow into each of those breasts on which his head had often reposed, in consequence of her falsehood and fascination; and, before she was dead, four wild horses were brought, and her arms and legs attached firmly, one to each, and then the horses were driven off, and Biswa Lukhy was torn to pieces.

Such was the story that, of all others, the queen my mistress delighted most to hear; and when the affectionate meeting of the prince and princess was described, with their happiness, I have seen the tears stand in her eyes with sympathy and joy.

And was not the end of Biswa Lukhy cruel? you ask, and was the fault altogether hers? No, the end of Biswa Lukhy was *not* cruel. She deserved it all, the vile slave, for keeping a prince and princess apart by her falsehood and her fascination, and the prince was quite right to put the poisoned arrows into her bosom, for was not her heart false? Inshallah! may all who act like her suffer like her!

Such is the end of Elihu Jan's story.

N

CHAPTER XVI.

OUDH became a kingdom in 1814. Before that, its sovereigns were styled nawabs. The first king, Ghazee-ood-deen Hyder, reigned from 1814 to 1827, and left in the treasury, at his death, ten millions of pounds sterling. His son, Nussir-ood-deen Hyder, some of whose doings are recorded in the 'Private Life of an Eastern King,' reigned from 1827 to 1837, and left in the treasury at his death about 700,000*l.* He had squandered not only the regular annual income of the kingdom on his pleasures and favourites, but also 9,300,000*l.* of the treasure accumulated by his father— that is, about a million a year in addition to the ordinary annual income. Nussir-ood-deen Hyder was succeeded by his uncle, Mohamed Aly Shah, who reigned from 1837 to 1842,

and left behind him in the treasury about
800,000*l.* His son, Umjid Aly Shah, consort of that queen whose life is illustrated in
these pages, reigned from 1842 to 1847, and
left behind him in the treasury 1,360,000*l.*
He was succeeded by his son Wajid Aly Shah,
now the ex-king of Oudh, who reigned till
the annexation of the country to the British
dominions in India in 1856.

The account given by Elihu Jan, in the
foregoing pages, of the palace life of Umjid
Aly Shah and Wajid Aly Shah, the two·last
kings of Oudh, is simple, plain, and unvar-
nished. In the present chapter I propose to
illustrate the same life from other sources,
and chiefly from Sir W. Sleeman's 'Journey
through the Kingdom of Oudh,' which was
published in London in 1858.

Sleeman, having been resident at the
court of Lucknow from 1849 to 1856, had
of course the best opportunity of becoming
acquainted with the state of the palace, and
the ordinary life of its principal inmates.
But his work was intended to serve a political purpose—his object was to show how

ruinous the misgovernment of the country had been—and consequently the 'Journey through the Kingdom of Oudh' is more taken up with the state of the provinces, the history of the leading families, and the conversations the resident held with the principal local authorities, than with the doings at court. These doings are, indeed, but incidentally introduced here and there, and hence the utility of collecting them together, to serve as an illustration of a state of society and of a court now probably for ever passed away.

In August 1849, writing to Lord Dalhousie, the resident gives the following account of Wajid Aly Shah, then the reigning sovereign : 'The king's habits will not alter. He was allowed by his father to associate, as at present he does, with singers from his boyhood, and he cannot endure the society of other persons. He no longer makes any attempt to conceal his determination to live exclusively in their society, and to hear and see nothing of what his officers do, or his people suffer. Whatever he has, he is ready to give to singers and eunuchs, or he allows them to take. No man

can take charge of any office without antici-
pating the income by large gratuities to them,
and the average gratuity which a contractor
for a year of a district yielding three lacs of
rupees annually (30,000*l*.), is made to pay
before he leaves the capital to enter upon his
charge, is estimated to be 50,000 rupees
(5,000*l*.).' And again, in the same letter:
'The king is utterly unfit to have anything
to do with the administration, since he has
never taken, or shown any wish to take, any
heed of what is done or suffered in the country. He spends all his time with singers and
the females they provide to amuse him, and
is for seven and eight hours together living in
the house of the chief singer, Rajee-ood-
Dowlah, a fellow who was only lately beating
a drum to a party of dancing girls, on some
four rupees a month. These singers are all
Domes, the lowest of the low castes of India,
and they and the eunuchs are now the virtual
sovereigns of the country.'

In the council of regency, which the
resident proposed, to supersede the king, the
king's mother—' the queen my mistress ' of

Elihu Jan's narrative—is mentioned first by Sir William, proving that she was a superior woman. The resolution which she formed to go to England after annexation, and the perseverance and energy with which she carried out that resolution, are sufficient to prove that the impression of the resident relative to her ability was correct.

In September 1849, writing to the Governor-General, the resident informs him in a postscript: ' I may mention that the king is now engaged in turning into verse a long prose history called " Hydree." About ten days ago all the poets of Lucknow were assembled at the palace to hear his majesty read his poem. They sat with him, listening to his, and reading their own, poems, from nine at night till three the next morning. One of the poets, the eldest son of a late minister, Aga Meen by name, told me *that the versification was exceedingly good for a king.* These are, I think, the only men, save the minister, the eunuchs, and the singers, who have had the honour of conversing with his majesty since I came here.'

In writing, during the same month, to Sir

H. M. Elliott he says : ' The king is in constant dread of poison, and would do anything to get relieved from that dread, and of all further importunity on the state of the country. His chief wife (Khash Mehal) would poison him to bring on the throne her son, and to restore to herself her paramour, who is now at Cawnpore waiting for some such change. Her uncle the minister would, the king thinks, be glad to see him poisoned, in the hope of having to conduct affairs during the minority. He is afraid to admonish his other chief wife for her infidelities with the chief favourite and singer, lest she should poison him to go off with her paramour to Rampore, whither he has sent the immense wealth that the king has lavished on him.'

Under date December 9, 1849, the resident writes : 'The king had several interviews with one Sadik Aly, who pretended to be the king of the fairies. His fairy majesty described the symptoms from which the king suffered, and prescribed remedies—these remedies consisting chiefly of rich offerings to the fairies, who were to relieve him. He

frequently received letters from the fairy king
to the same effect, written in an imperious
style suited to the occasion. The farce was
carried on for several months, and the king
at different times is supposed to have given
this Sadik Aly some two lacs of rupees
(20,000*l.*), which he shared with the singers.'

In the same month the king, having become
convinced of the knavery of this Sadik Aly,
and of the fact of the chief singer and others
of his court having been accomplices, promised Captain Bird, the assistant-resident,
that he would banish the culprits across the
Ganges. As the king seemed in no hurry,
however, to perform this promise, Captain
Bird demanded an audience, and was at first
refused, the king pleading indisposition. Ul-
timately the demand was complied with, and
Captain Bird, on being introduced, found the
king in a small inner room of the palace,
lying on a cot covered with a quilt or ruzaie.
There were closed doors on the side of the
room where the cot was placed, and Captain
Bird perceived that persons were listening to
the conversation. On the minister advancing

to meet him at the door, Captain Bird declined to take his hand, saying 'I believe you are an accomplice of these fiddlers, and are afraid to have them removed, or else his majesty's orders would have been carried out before this.' Captain Bird then advanced to the king, and shook hands with him, when the following conversation took place :—

Capt. Bird. I have come to claim the fulfilment of your majesty's promise to dismiss the singers, Gholam Ruza and his sister, and Kotub Aly, and to send them across the Ganges.

The King. I never gave any such promise.

Capt. Bird. Your majesty's promise was given in the following words. (Captain Bird here read the court news-writer's report of the same.)

The king is uneasy, and apparently at a loss for an answer.

The Minister. His majesty has ascertained from the confession of Sadik Aly himself that Gholam Ruza and his sister are innocent in this matter.

Capt. Bird. His majesty told me that

the deception had been so fully proved that they were speechless; and further, that his majesty had thereupon spit in their faces.

The King. No, not in Gholam Ruza's. His sister and Kotub Aly are alone guilty.

Capt. Bird. If these parties are not removed, according to your majesty's promise, all Lucknow will say that I have been bribed to permit them to remain.

The King. That is all nonsense. Do you want me to swear that Gholam Ruza is inno cent, and that I never gave the promise you mention?

Then, calling the minister, the king placed his right hand on the minister's head and said, 'I swear, as if this were my son's head, and by God, that I believe Gholam Ruza to be entirely innocent; and that I never promised to turn him out, or banish him beyond the Ganges.

Capt. Bird. Your majesty has, at all events, acknowledged the guilt of Gholam Ruza's sister, and of Kotub Aly. Let punishment be executed on the guilty.

The King. When absent from my sight,

.they are as far off as if they were across a hundred rivers. I know they are intriguers. I shall keep my eye on them.

Capt. Bird. I have reported this case officially. Your majesty has made me a participator in the breaking of your word.

The King. This case has reference only to my own household, not to the government; but if you wish to use force, take me by the beard, and pull me from the throne.

Capt. Bird. Often when force might have been used, under your own sign-manual, on these fiddlers interfering in state affairs, the resident has forborne. Now, who can be your friend, or save you from danger? I must report all to the resident.

The King. Yes. Report that the king has changed his mind, broken his word, and will not fulfil his promise. Ask for permission to employ force for the removal of these men, and see if he will permit it.

Captain Bird shortly after took his leave, and next day Sadik Aly, the pretended king of the fairies, had a dress of honour conferred upon him by the king, and a hundred rupees a month added to his salary. Gholam Ruza and a relative of his were seated behind his majesty, in his carriage and four, the same evening, driving through the streets of Lucknow.

Six months afterwards, however, in May 1850, the king had fourteen fiddlers and singers, amongst whom were Gholam Ruza, his father, sister, and brother, seized and imprisoned, and shortly after banished them across the Ganges, taking from them all the wealth they had retained in Lucknow, for they had sent the greater part out of Oudh. The immediate cause of this banishment was the king's having found out that his divorced wife, Surfraz Muhal, was living with the chief singer, Gholam Ruza.

Captain Bird was afterwards a strenuous opposer of the annexation of Oudh, and agent in England for the ex-king. He was in attendance on the queen dowager of Oudh when she visited England.

The following scene is highly characteristic, and is certainly as extravagant as anything related by Elihu Jan :—

'In the beginning of Sept. 1850, the king became enamoured of one of his mother's waiting-maids, and demanded her in marriage. She was his mother's favourite bedfellow, and his mother would not part with her. The king became angry, and to soothe him, his mother told him it was purely out of regard for him and his children that she refused to part with this young woman, as she had a *sampun*, or the coiled figure of a snake, under the hair on the back of her neck. No man will purchase a horse with such a mark, or believe that any family can be safe in which a horse or mare with such a mark is kept. His mother told him, that, if he cohabited with a woman having such a mark, he and all his children would perish.

'The king then said that he might probably have, among his many wives, some with marks of this kind, and that this might account for his frequent attacks of palpitation of the heart. "No doubt," said the queen dowager. "We have long thought so; but your majesty gets into such a towering passion when we venture to speak of your wives, that we have been afraid to give expression to our thoughts and fears." "Perhaps, said the king, 'I may owe to this cause the death, lately, of my poor son, the heir apparent." "We have long thought so," said the queen.

'The chief eunuch, Busheer, was forthwith ordered to inspect the back of the necks of all, save that of the chief consort, mother of the late and present heir apparent.

'He reported that he had found the fatal mark upon the necks of no less than eight of the king's wives—to wit, Nishat Mehal, Koorshed Mehal, Soleman Mehal, Huzrut Mehal, Dara Begum, Buree Begum, Chotee Begum, and Huzrut Begum. The chief priest was summoned, and divorce from the whole eight pronounced forthwith; and the ladies were ordered to depart, with all that they had saved whilst in the palace. Some of their friends suggested that Mohammedans were but unskilful judges in such matters, and that a court of Brahmans should be assembled, as they had whole volumes devoted exclusively to this science.

'The most learned Brahmans were accordingly collected, and they declared that, though there were marks resembling in some degree the *sampun*, it was of no importance, and the evil threatened might be averted by singeing the head of the snake with a hot iron. The ladies were very indignant, and six of them insisted upon leaving the palace forthwith, in virtue of the divorce. Two only consented to remain, the Buree and Chotee Begums.' *

One of the six thus divorced, Huzrut Mehal, was the mother of that Brijis Kudr, son of the king, whom the rebels proclaimed king of Oudh during the mutiny, notwithstanding her opposition. She is now living in Nepaul, and lately got a village from Jung Bahadur, yielding her about 4,000 rupees a year.

The following is an English lady's description of two beauties of the court of Oudh, and is taken from Mrs. Park's 'Wanderings,' vol. i. p. 87 : 'The king's wives were superbly dressed, and looked like creatures of the Arabian tales. One, Taj Mehal, was so beautiful, that I could think of nothing but Lalla

* Sleeman's Journey, vol. i. p. 107.

Rookh in her bridal attire. I never saw anyone so lovely, either black or white. Her features were perfect, and such eyes and eyelashes I never beheld before. At present she appears to be the favourite, and is about fourteen years of age. She is a little creature, with the smallest hands and feet, and the most timid modest look imaginable. You would have been charmed with her, she is so graceful and swanlike.

' Her dress was of gold and scarlet brocade, and her hair was literally strewed with pearls, which hung down upon her neck in long single strings, terminating in large pearls, which mixed with and hung as low as her hair, which was curled on each side of her head in long ringlets, like the beauties of the court of Charles II. On her forehead she wore a small gold circlet, from which depended and hung, half-way down, large pearls, interspersed with emeralds. Above this was a bird of paradise plume, from which strings of pearls were carried over the head, as we turn back our hair.

' Her earrings were immense gold rings,

with pearls and emeralds suspended all round in large strings, the pearls increasing in size, towards the centre. She had a nose-ring also, with large round pearls and emeralds, and her necklaces &c., were too numerous to be described.

'She wore long sleeves, open at the elbow; and her dress was a full petticoat, with a tight body attached, and open only at the throat. She had several attendants to bear her train when she walked; and her women stood behind her couch to arrange her head-dress, when, in moving, the strings of pearls got entangled in the immense robe of scarlet and gold she had thrown around her. This beautiful creature is the envy of all the other wives, and the favourite at present both of the king and his mother, both of whom have given her titles of honour.

'The other newly-made queen is nearly European, but not a whit fairer than Taj Mehal. She is, in my opinion, plain; but by the native ladies she is considered very handsome. She was the king's favourite before he saw Taj Mehal. Her head-dress was a

o

coronet of diamonds, with a fine crescent and plume of the same. She is the daughter of a European merchant, and is accomplished for the inhabitant of a zenana, as she writes and speaks Persian fluently, as well as Hindustanee. It is said that she is teaching the king English, though when we spoke to her in English, she said she had forgotten it, and could not reply in that language. She was, I fancy, afraid of the queen dowager, as she evidently understood us, and when asked if she liked being in the harem, she shook her head and looked quite melancholy. Jealousy of the new favourite, however, appeared to be the cause of her discontent, as, though they sat on the same couch, they never addressed each other.

'The mother of the king's children, and of the heir-apparent, did not visit us at the queen dowager's; but we went to see her at her own palace. She is, after all, the consort of most political importance, and, it is said, has great power over her royal husband, whose ears she sometimes boxes soundly.'

So much for the inner life of the palace;

and now, with a few observations on the way in which business was transacted in the court of the ex-king, and the state of the country under him, I shall conclude. If anyone can have a doubt as to the expediency of having annexed a country, the government of which was so frightfully mismanaged, let him consider calmly the picture here presented, and then reflect that Oudh, at the present moment, is one of the most peaceful, quiet, orderly, and best-governed countries in India, advancing rapidly in a career of development of its natural resources, and of internal improvement—so rapidly, indeed, that where, eight years ago, all was confusion, lawlessness, rapine, and violence, roads are now being constructed, navigable rivers opened up to trade, the country can be traversed from one end to the other with the same security as the traveller journeys in England, and law and justice are supreme.

It might be supposed that, if the king himself did not transact the public business when he was upon the throne, at least his vizier or prime minister did. Such, however, was not the case. The vizier put neither his seal nor signature on any public orders. Probably, fear of the caprice which dictated all the proceedings of the king, and fear of the intrigues of the palace, were the causes of this strange omission. The only thing in the vizier's handwriting, when an order was passed, was the figure indicating the date, or day of the month. During times of festivity and religious fasts, papers accumulated to such an extent, that a miscellaneous bundle was tied up by a string, and the vizier put the figure indicating the day of the month, outside, once for all, and then his deputies, favourites, or secretaries, passed the orders. Nothing but the figure, in the vizier's handwriting, attested the genuineness of the order, and that figure he himself could not truly swear to in a month. Thus, he could always repudiate any order that turned out to be obnoxious, and the writer of it would probably be warned in time to make his escape.

These deputies, favourites, and secretaries of the vizier were of course perfectly aware

of the large sums of money which he ille-
gally received as gratuities, or *nuzzeranas*,
and they took care that further exactions
were made on their own account. Thus, all
were bound together by a common interest,
and they well knew that, although they
might be in disgrace one day, their turn
would come again after a little, when the
storm had blown over, and their offence was
forgotten.

In October 1850 Hussun Khan, one of
the king's pages, whose duty it was to sub-
mit letters and documents to the king, fell
under his majesty's displeasure, and his estate
was confiscated, and his house searched.
Amongst his papers, several of the resident's
official notes to the king were found un-
opened, some of them marked 'emergent.'
Now, it must be evident that Hussun Khan
found the evil of not delivering such letters
the less evil of the two—the anger of an un-
principled tyrant falling usually in the first
instance on the bearer of unpleasant tidings.

Under former sovereigns, from ten to
fifteen per cent. of the net collections of

revenue found their way into the hands of the minister and his satellites; but, under the reign of Wajid Aly, not less than twenty-five per cent. were thus embezzled; and, in fact, things were coming to such a pass in Lucknow, that, although his father left in the treasury nearly a million and a half of money, on his death, in 1847, the ex-king was deeply embarrassed as early as 1850— all the revenue and all the savings in the treasury having been spent, and no money forthcoming to pay troops or public servants of any kind, except those in immediate attendance on the court.

'Under the present wretched system,' wrote Sir W. Sleeman in 1851, 'the contractors who have the farm of the revenue let out districts to subordinate officers, who abuse their authority as much as contractors and court favourites abuse theirs, and commit all kinds of outrages on the unoffending people. Security to life and property is disregarded, and is unknown.' *

And again he writes: 'In this overgrown

* Journey through Oudh, vol. i. p. 202.

city (Lucknow) there is a perpetual turmoil of processions, illuminations, and festivities. The sovereign spends all that he can get on them, and has not the slightest wish to perpetuate his name by the construction of any useful or even ornamental work beyond its suburbs. All the members of his family, and of the city aristocracy, follow his example, and spend their means in the same way. Utterly indifferent to the feelings and opinions of the landed aristocracy and the people of the country, with whom they have no sympathy whatever, they spend all that they can obtain from the public in gratifying the vitiated tastes of the overgrown metropolis. The king is utterly indifferent to the duties and responsibilities of his high office, and to the sufferings of the many millions subject to his rule. His time and attention are devoted entirely to the pursuit of personal gratifications. He associates with none but such as contribute to such gratification—women, singers, fiddlers, and eunuchs. He never, I believe, reads or hears any petition from his suffering people, any report from his local officers, civil or military, or, in fact, functionaries of any kind. He takes no interest whatever in public affairs, and appears to care nothing whatever about them.'

When such was the state of the court, and of Lucknow, it may be easily conceived what the condition of the more remote districts of the country was. Fortunately, however, we are not left to conjecture in this matter. In 1850 and 1851, Sir W. Sleeman himself went through the country, saw everything with his own eyes, and has left on record the results of his inspection. The following details, relative to the sufferings of the agricultural population, are partly drawn from Sir William's narrative, and partly derived from information I have myself received from the villagers in going through the country on official tours.

In the Durriabad district, Bhooree Khan was one of the most notorious leaders of robbers and dacoits, from 1846 to 1851, and the government was unable or unwilling to punish his misconduct. In 1848, he attacked a village in the neighbourhood of Redowly, and, having driven off a hundred and fifty head of cattle, he seized Ousan, an Upuddhya Brahman, and Peer Khan, a Mussulman, two of the wealthiest inhabitants, with their sons, in order to extort ransom from them. Ousan's ransom was fixed at 1,200 rupees (120*l*.), and Peer Khan's at 800 rupees (80*l*.). Ousan himself was let go in order that he might raise the money, whilst his two sons, fourteen and sixteen years of age respectively, were retained as hostages. Ousan could only raise 700 rupees (70*l*.), which amount he sent. Bhooree Khan was not satisfied, and, on the expiration of the time allowed, brought out the two boys, half starved, from their place of confinement, with fetters on their legs, and bamboo collars round their necks. Having tied them to two trees, he and his band shot at them with bows and arrows, and left them so to die.

Peer Khan had no sons; but his two younger brothers were seized as hostages, whilst the unfortunate man himself was allowed to go to procure the amount of

ransom. As this amount was not forthcoming at the appointed time, Bhooree Khan
had the two young men beaten with sticks,
iron spikes driven up under their nails, their
eyelids sewn up with needle and thread,
their beards burned off with lighted flam-
beaux, and other tortures inflicted that cannot be particularised. Next day, Peer Khan
brought the amount, 800 rupees, and his
brothers, more dead than alive, were released. One of them died a day or two
afterwards of the sufferings he had endured;
the other lived, impotent and a cripple.

This same Bhooree Khan next year attacked the house of Dulla, the most opulent
merchant of Muhdoompore, and succeeded in
seizing his son Nychint, and his grandson,
son of Nychint, Ajoodhya by name. The
females of the family fortunately escaped,
and the robbers could not find the treasures
of which they were in search, but which
they knew were buried somewhere in or
near the house. A Brahman, named Cheyn,
who knew Dulla, and knew also where the
treasure was buried, was also made prisoner.

Next day, Bhooree Khan brought forth Nychint, and ordered him to point out where the valuables were buried. This he would not do, and Bhooree Khan had four tent-pegs driven into the ground, placed Nychint on his face on the ground, and had his feet and hands tied to the pegs. He then had the unfortunate prisoner burnt to the bone in several places with red-hot ramrods, but Nychint still refused to point out the treasure.

A large brass vessel of oil was then heated to the boiling-point, and the boiling oil was poured over Nychint's body—the skin peeling off, and the poor sufferer becoming insensible. When Nychint recovered his senses, he pointed out the spot. Property in gold, silver, brass vessels, and grain, to the amount of 150,000 rupees (15,000*l.*), is said to have been carried off by the freebooter. Nychint was unbound and released, but died the same night.

Such narratives might be indefinitely multiplied, with more horrible tales of torture inflicted upon unoffending women and girls, but I refrain. In commenting on this history of Bhooree Khan, Sir W. Sleeman writes: 'An Englishman may ask how it is that a wretch guilty of such cruelties to men who have never injured him, to innocent and unoffending women and children, can find, in a society where slavery is not recognised, men to assist him in inflicting them, and landholders of high rank and large possessions to screen and shelter him when pursued by government. For a solution of this problem he must go back to the middle ages, in England and the other nations of Europe, when the baronial proprietors of the soil, too strong for their sovereigns, committed the same cruelties, found the same willing instruments in their retainers, and members of the same class of landed proprietors, to screen, shelter and encourage them in their iniquities.

'They acquiesce in the atrocities committed by one who is in armed opposition to the government to-day, and they aid him in his enterprises, openly or secretly, because they know that they may be in the same condition, and require the same aid from him to-morrow; that the more sturdy the resistance made by one, the less likely will the government officers be to rouse the resistance of the others. They do not sympathise with those who suffer from his depredations, or aid the government officers in protecting them, because they know that they could not support the means required to enable them successfully to contend with their sovereign and reduce him to terms, without plundering and occasionally murdering the innocent of all ages and both sexes, and that they may have to raise the same means for a similar contest to-morrow. They are satisfied, therefore, if they can save their own tenants from pillage and slaughter. They find moreover that the sufferings of others enable them to get cultivators and useful tenants of all kinds upon their own estates on easier terms; whilst it induces the smaller proprietors around to yield up their lands and become their tenants with less difficulty. It was in the same manner that the great feudal barons aggrandised themselves in England, and in the other countries of Europe, in the middle ages.

Happily this state of things is now at an end. The large landholders know that they cannot resist the power of the British government. They have been conciliated by judicious concessions, their estates guaranteed to them in perpetuity, and many of them have been invested with judicial powers, which they exercise, for the most part, with judgment and discretion. That one or two of them should have abused their power, and endeavoured to use that as an instrument of oppression which was granted for the public good, was but to be expected in the nature of things. But that the country has entered upon a career of prosperity, which, if peace be continued, will soon render it the garden of India, is undoubted.

In the mean time, the folly of the ex-king and his court continues as great as ever. His palace, at Garden Reach in Calcutta, is the Alsatia of India, and the following extract from a late number of the Calcutta 'Hurkaru' newspaper (May 1864) shows that the career of insensate folly commened in Lucknow, when ruling an extensive country, continues unabated in the comparative retirement of his pensioned idleness :—

'The ex-king of Oudh has, with the pious resignation of ancient heroes, subsided into the happy and contented enjoyment of his present state. His majesty's time is equally divided between religious exercises, which he has never neglected, even during his worst days, and the care and collection of wild animals of every kind. It is true that the royal tastes are occasionally rather expensive, subjecting the royal exchequer to sudden and extraordinary demands, and the accountant-general of the royal revenues to cruel embarrassments. But the pursuit of knowledge, even under difficulties, is held to be laudable, and there are those about his Majesty's person who take care that his love of nature shall never lack encouragement and gratification.

'We do not know whether they belong to the scientific society recently established by an enterprising and learned moolvie of Ghazeepore, which boasts the duke of Argyle for its president and patron, and which dedicates its books to his grace. But the zeal with which they keep alive the royal devotion to natural history, within the purlieus of Garden Reach, entitles them to any distinction within the power of the society to confer.

'It is nothing unusual for them to present his majesty with a pair of peacocks, purchased for thirty thousand rupees (3,000*l.*); or a cage of canaries of a remarkable description, for half a lac of rupees (5,000*l.*).

'It is enough that a beast or a bird, even of the commonest kind, should have some unusual mark or feature about it, so as to be quite unlike others of the same species, and it obtains a place at once in the royal menagerie, and displaces some thousands of rupees from the royal treasure-chests.

'The other day, a pair of vultures, a species of bird remarkable for the beauty and richness of their plumage, and the gracefulness of their movements, were brought before the ex-king, and a warty excrescence on the head of each—certainly improving their appearance—was pointed out. The creatures were hugely admired, and the man who brought them was asked to name his price. " Fifty thousand rupees " (5,000*l.*). " Fifty thousand rupees! well, let it be fifty thousand," and the accountant-general was ordered to pay up. But that high dignitary found no more than thirty-five thousand in the royal treasury, and that amount was ordinarily retained, as a reserve fund, to meet extraordinary calls. This faithful servant therefore demurred to parting with the last rupee before the next pay-day. He was alternately laughed and frowned out of his scruples, and the entire amount went in part payment for the vultures.

'But there remained a balance of fifteen thousand rupees (1,500*l.*) to be paid, and neither cash nor credit was to be had.

'In this dilemma, one of the two golden bedsteads, made during the reign of the great Saadut Aly Khan, was broken up, melted down, and the balance paid.

'These matters are not intruded on the public out of an idle passion for gossip. They prove how much philosophy may do to reconcile one to the loss of a throne and kingdom; and truly thankful the tax-payers of India ought to be that, under the enlightened and strictly honest guiding of the courtiers, by whom the ex-king is surrounded, his majesty is making such excellent use of their money.'

The ex-king's pension is a lac of rupees a month, or 120,000*l.* a year.

LONDON
PRINTED BY SPOTTISWOODE AND CO.
NEW-STREET SQUARE